Thank you!

BELMONT COUNTY DISTRICT LIBRARY
Purchased with funds from the
November 2013 Library Levy

MARY SHELLEY'S

FRANKENSTEIN

A GRAPHIC NOVEL
BY MICHAEL BURGAN &
DENNIS CALERO

STONE ARCH BOOKS
A CAPSTONE IMPRINT

Graphic Revolve is published by Stone Arch Books
A Capstone Imprint
1710 Roe Crest Drive, North Mankato, Minnesota 56003
www.capstonepub.com

Cataloging-in-Publication Data is available at the Library
of Congress website.
Hardcover ISBN: 978-1-4965-0009-0
Paperback ISBN: 978-1-4965-0028-1

Summary: The young scientist Victor Frankenstein
has created something amazing and horrible at the
same time — a living being out of dead flesh and bone.
His creation, however, turns out to be a monster.
Frankenstein's creation quickly discovers that his hideous
appearance frightens away any companions. Now Victor
Frankenstein must stop his creation before the monster's
loneliness turns to violence.

Common Core back matter written by Dr. Katie Monnin.

Designer: Bob Lentz
Assistant Designer: Peggie Carley
Editor: Donald Lemke
Assistant Editor: Sean Tulien
Creative Director: Heather Kindseth
Editorial Director: Michael Dahl
Publisher: Ashley C. Andersen Zantop

Printed in the United States of America in
Stevens Point, Wisconsin.
052014   008092WZF14

TABLE OF CONTENTS

ABOUT FRANKENSTEIN'S MONSTER

The idea for *Frankenstein* came from a dream! One night in 1816, Mary Shelley and other authors decided to have a ghost story contest. At first, Shelley couldn't think of an idea. That evening, however, she dreamed about a frightening monster. The very next day she started writing her famous novel.

Shelly wasn't the only author in the ghost story contest to create a famous monster. John Polidori started writing a book called *The Vampyre*. Even today, most vampires are modeled after Polidori's version.

In 1818, the first edition of *Frankenstein* was published in three parts and didn't include Shelley's name. The author's name didn't appear on the cover until the second edition, published in 1823.

Many people who have not read the book believe that Shelley named her monster Frankenstein. In fact, she never gave the monster a name. Frankenstein is the last name of the doctor who created the monster.

The first film about the monster was shown in 1910. Like other films during this time, the movie didn't have any sound. It was also only 12 minutes long.

Many people imagine Frankenstein's monster with bolts in his neck, stitches across his forehead, and green skin. However, the monster's looks have changed many times. The image often used on Halloween masks became famous in 1931 when the actor Boris Karloff played the monster in the movie *Frankenstein*.

Frankenstein's monster has starred in hundreds of other films, TV shows, and comic books. Today, Shelley's creation continues to frighten people of all ages.

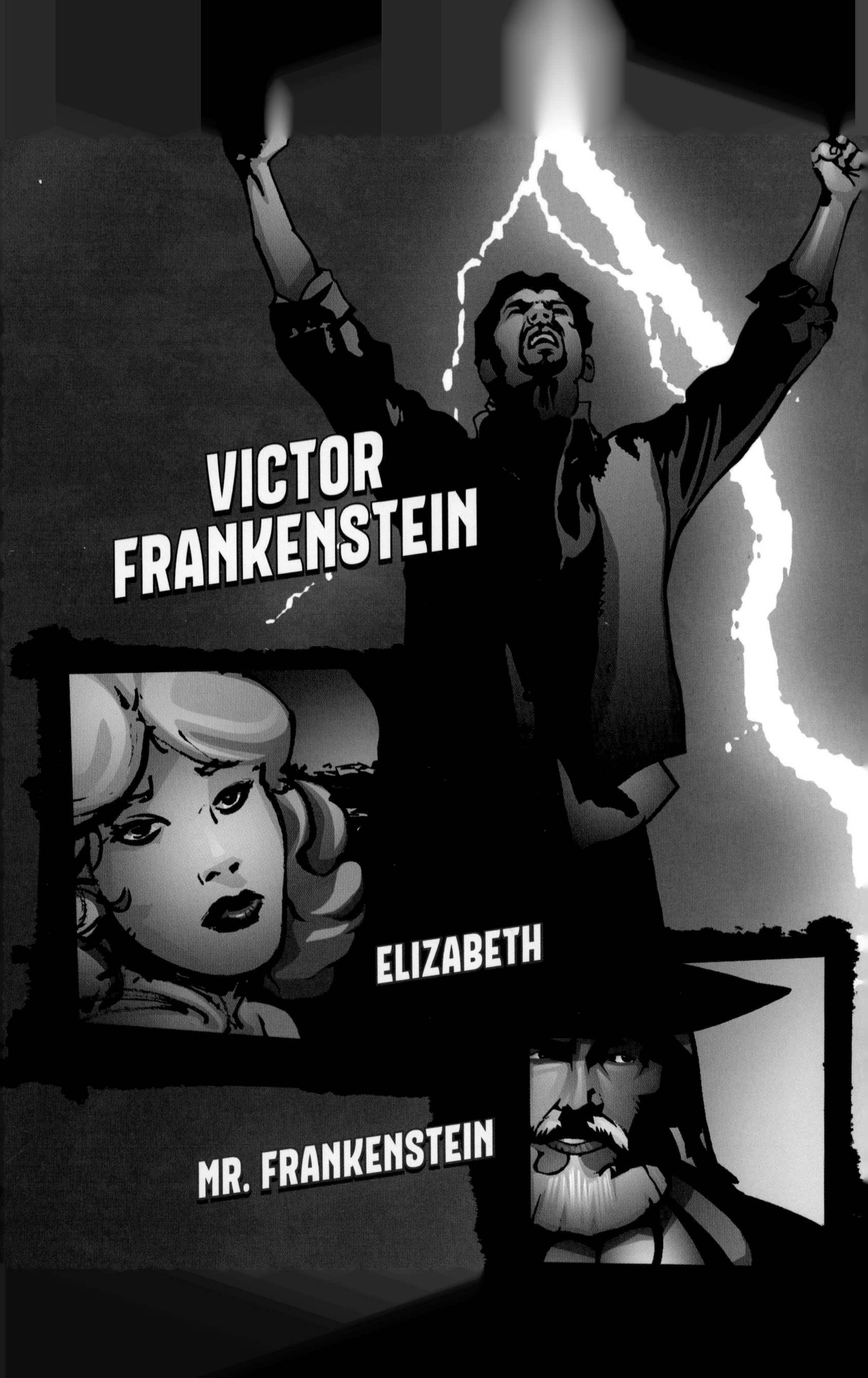
VICTOR FRANKENSTEIN
ELIZABETH
MR. FRANKENSTEIN

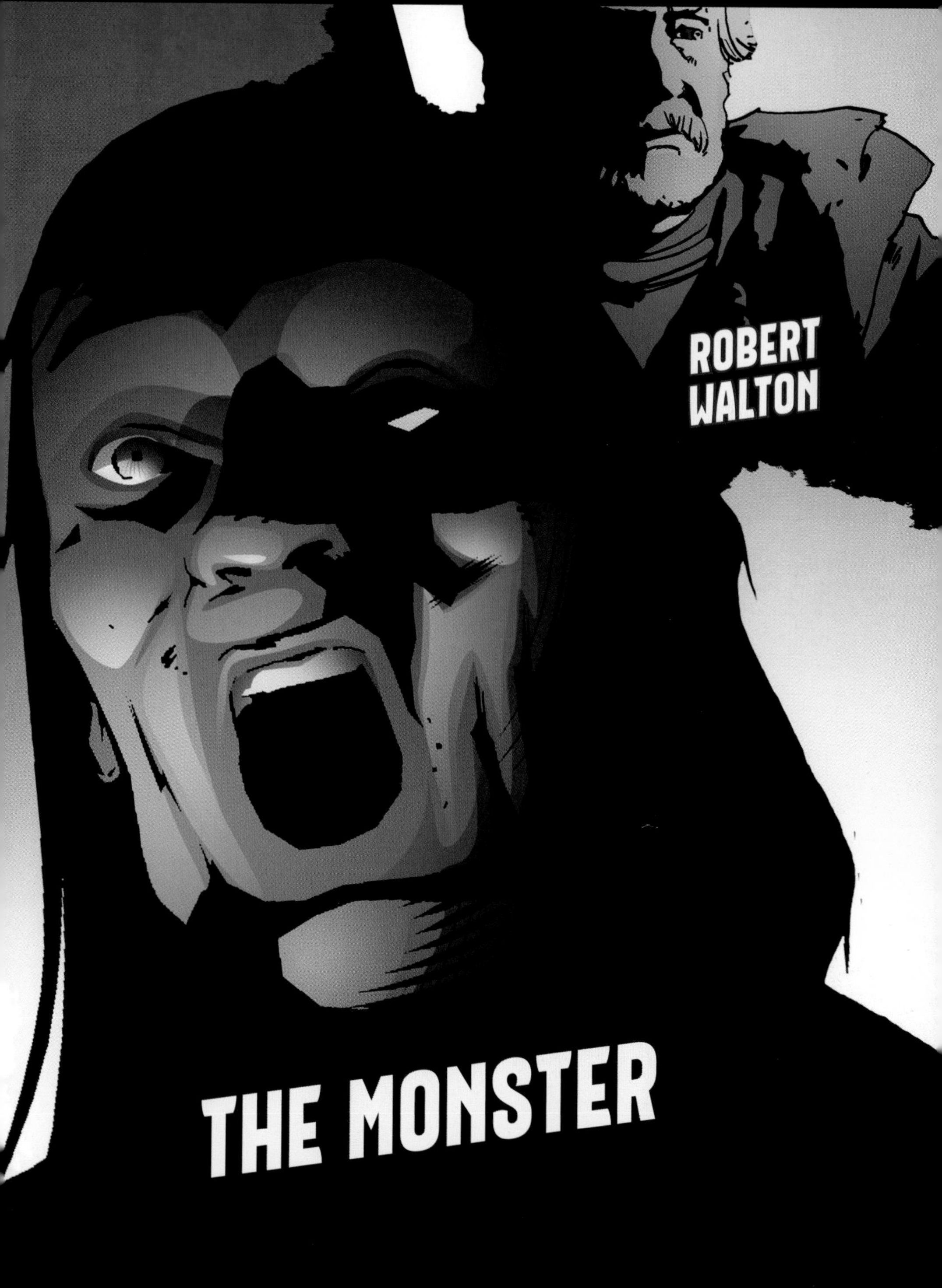
ROBERT
WALTON
THE MONSTER

CHAPTER 1
MYSTERY ON THE ICE

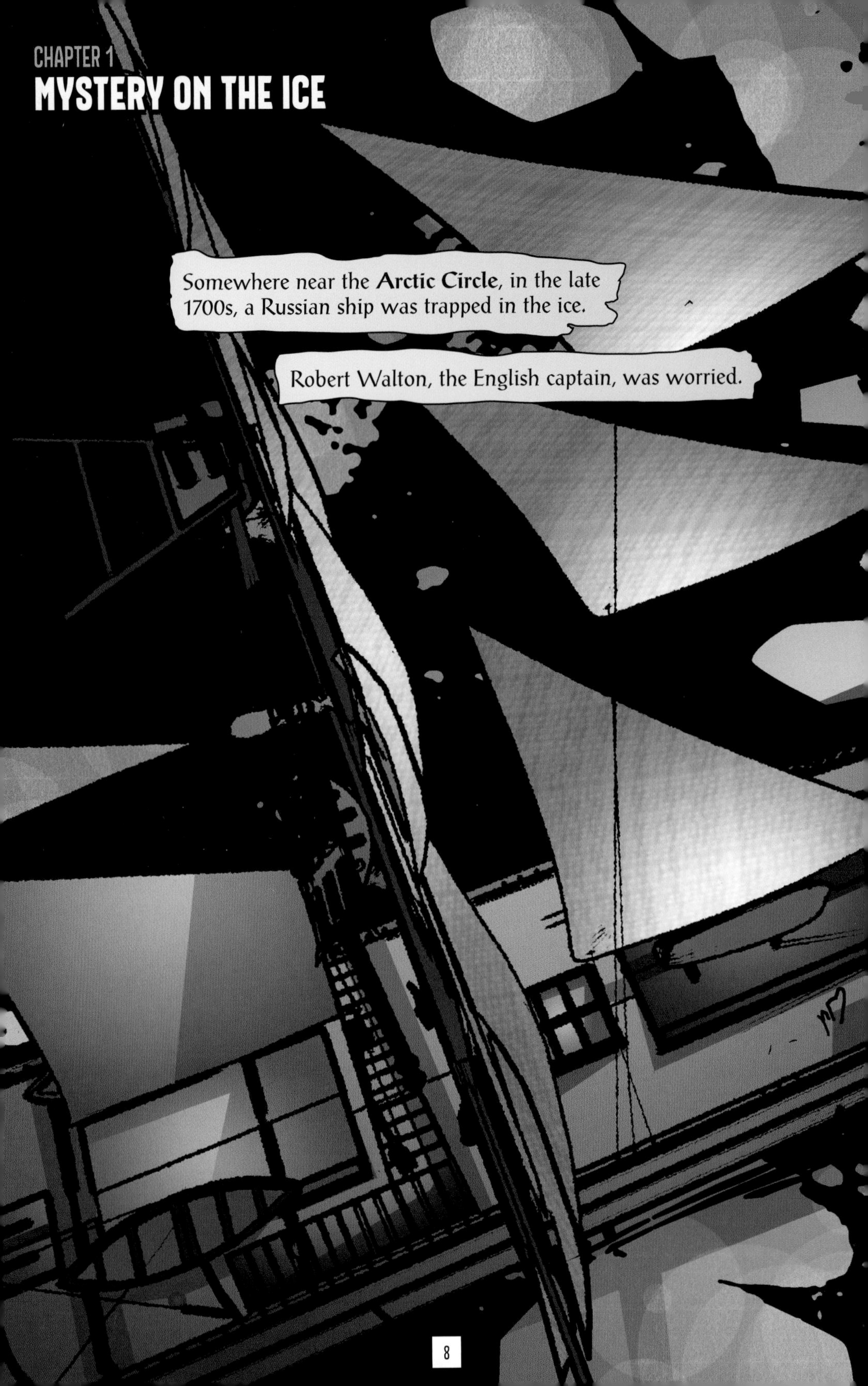
Somewhere near the **Arctic Circle**, in the late 1700s, a Russian ship was trapped in the ice.
Robert Walton, the English captain, was worried.

We can't move. The ice is too thick. We'll never reach the North Pole!

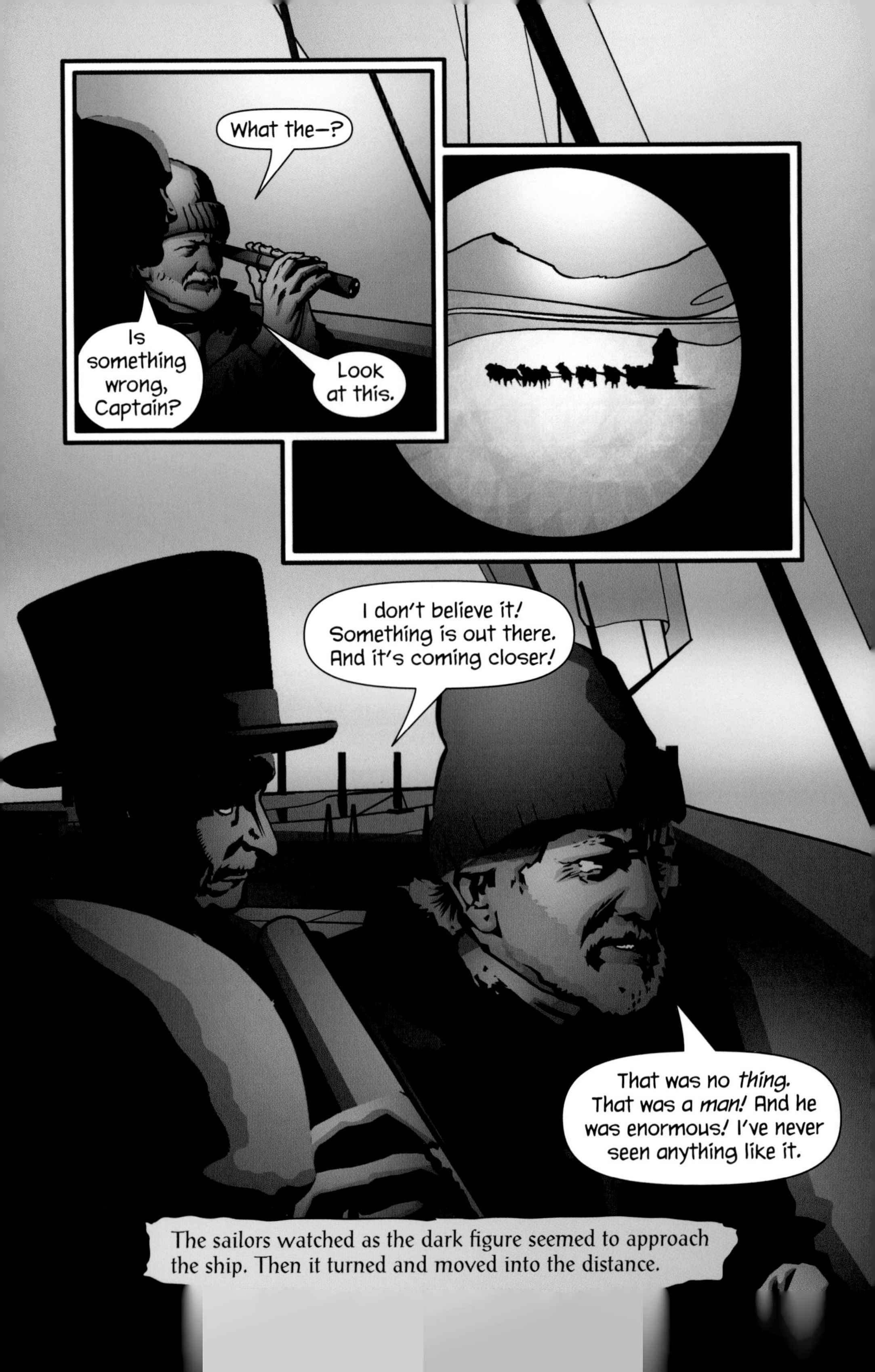
What the—?
Is something wrong, Captain?
Look at this.
I don't believe it! Something is out there. And it's coming closer!
That was no *thing*. That was a *man!* And he was enormous! I've never seen anything like it.

The sailors watched as the dark figure seemed to approach the ship. Then it turned and moved into the distance.

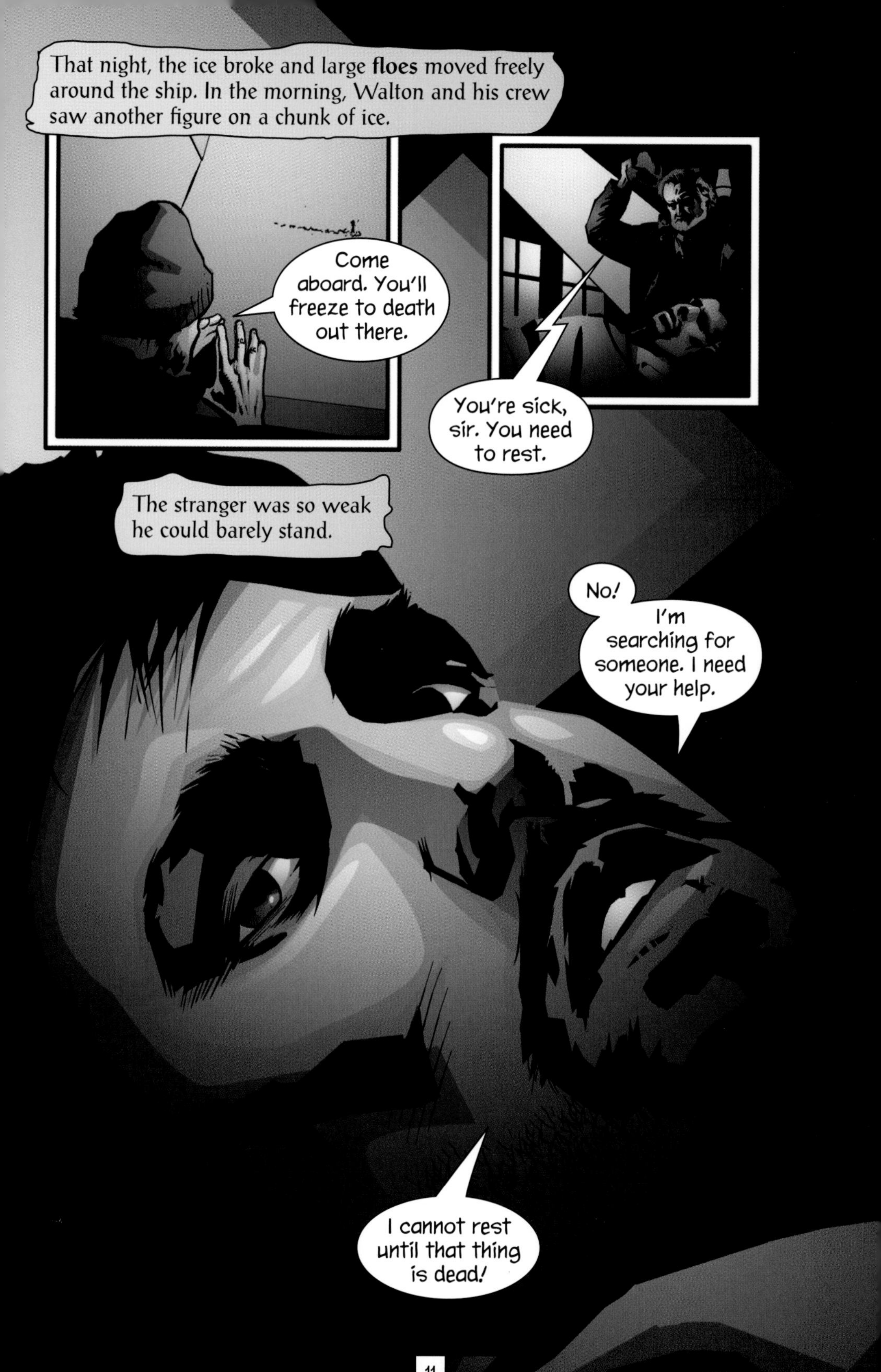

That night, the ice broke and large **floes** moved freely around the ship. In the morning, Walton and his crew saw another figure on a chunk of ice.
Come aboard. You'll freeze to death out there.
You're sick, sir. You need to rest.
The stranger was so weak he could barely stand.
No!
I'm searching for someone. I need your help.
I cannot rest until that thing is dead!

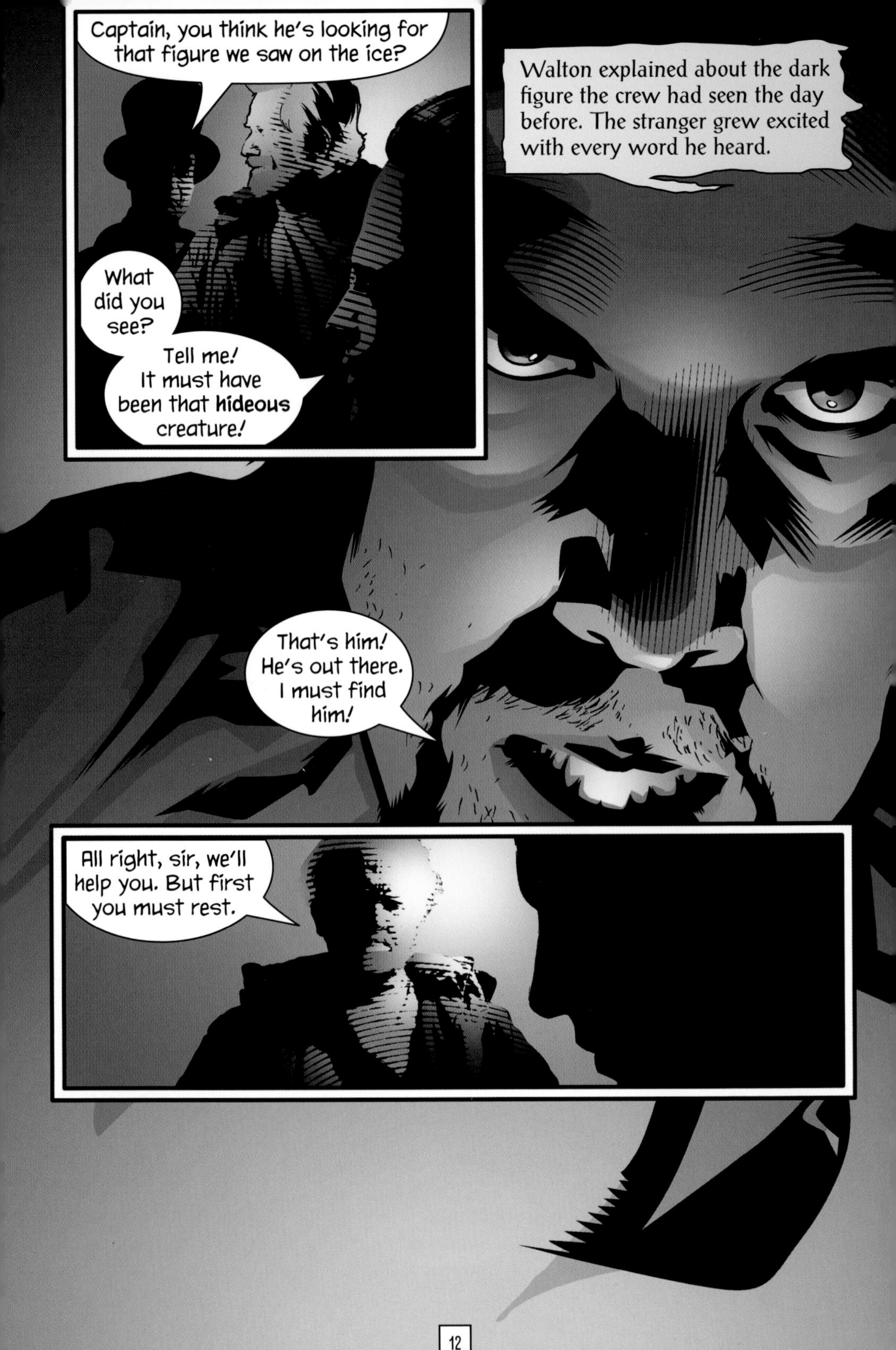

Captain, you think he's looking for that figure we saw on the ice?
Walton explained about the dark figure the crew had seen the day before. The stranger grew excited with every word he heard.
What did you see?
Tell me! It must have been that **hideous** creature!
That's him! He's out there. I must find him!
All right, sir, we'll help you. But first you must rest.

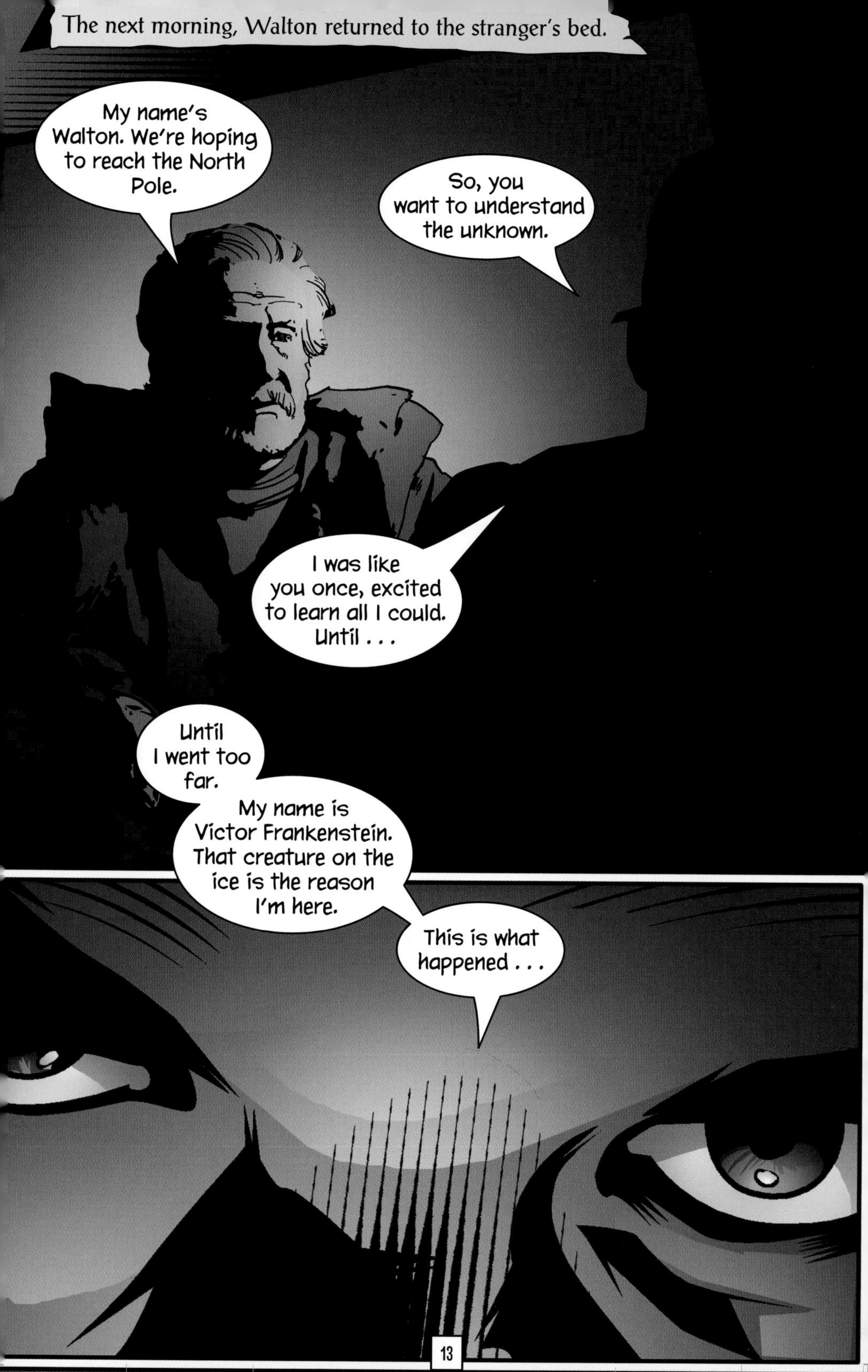
The next morning, Walton returned to the stranger's bed.
My name's Walton. We're hoping to reach the North Pole.
So, you want to understand the unknown.
I was like you once, excited to learn all I could. Until . . .
Until I went too far.
My name is Victor Frankenstein. That creature on the ice is the reason I'm here.
This is what happened . . .

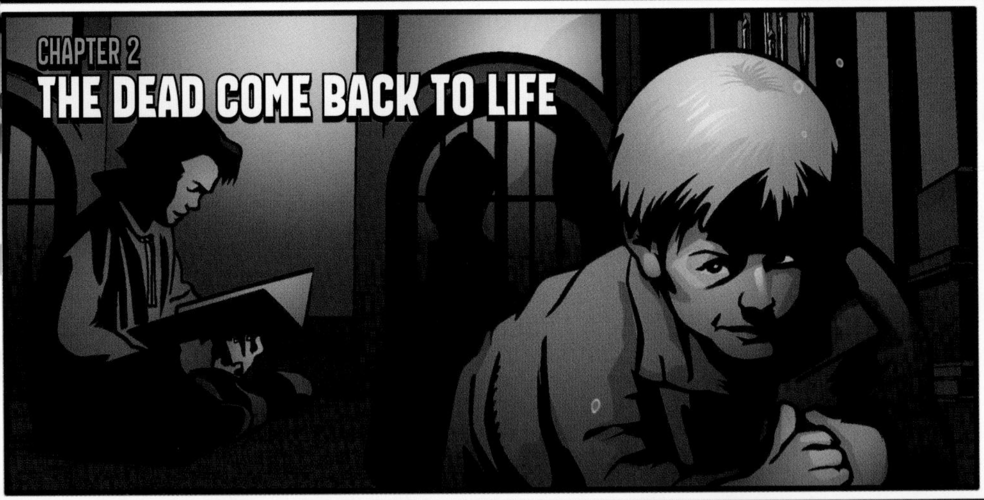
CHAPTER 2
THE DEAD COME BACK TO LIFE

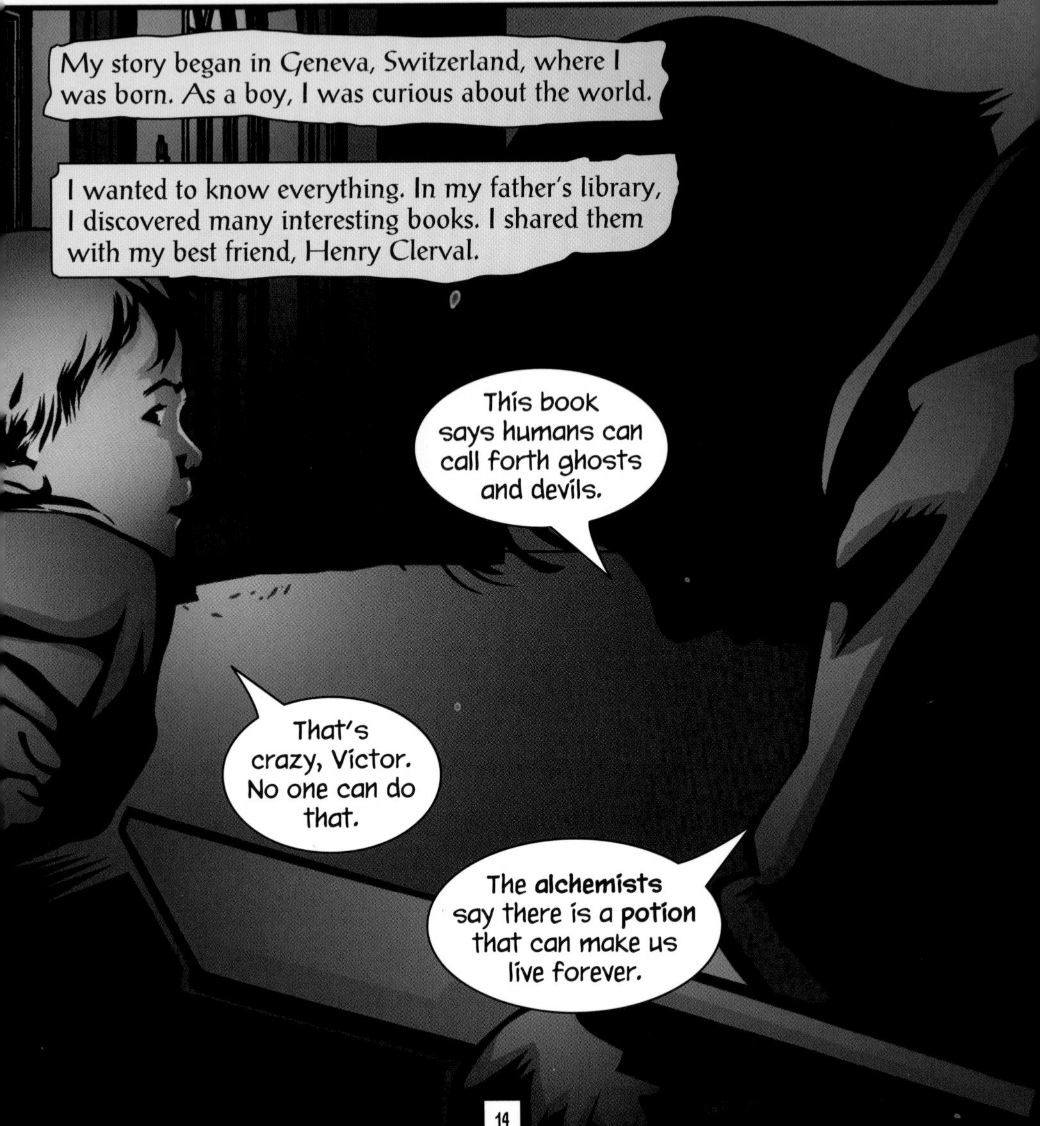
My story began in Geneva, Switzerland, where I was born. As a boy, I was curious about the world.
I wanted to know everything. In my father's library, I discovered many interesting books. I shared them with my best friend, Henry Clerval.
This book says humans can call forth ghosts and devils.
That's crazy, Victor. No one can do that.
The alchemists say there is a potion that can make us live forever.

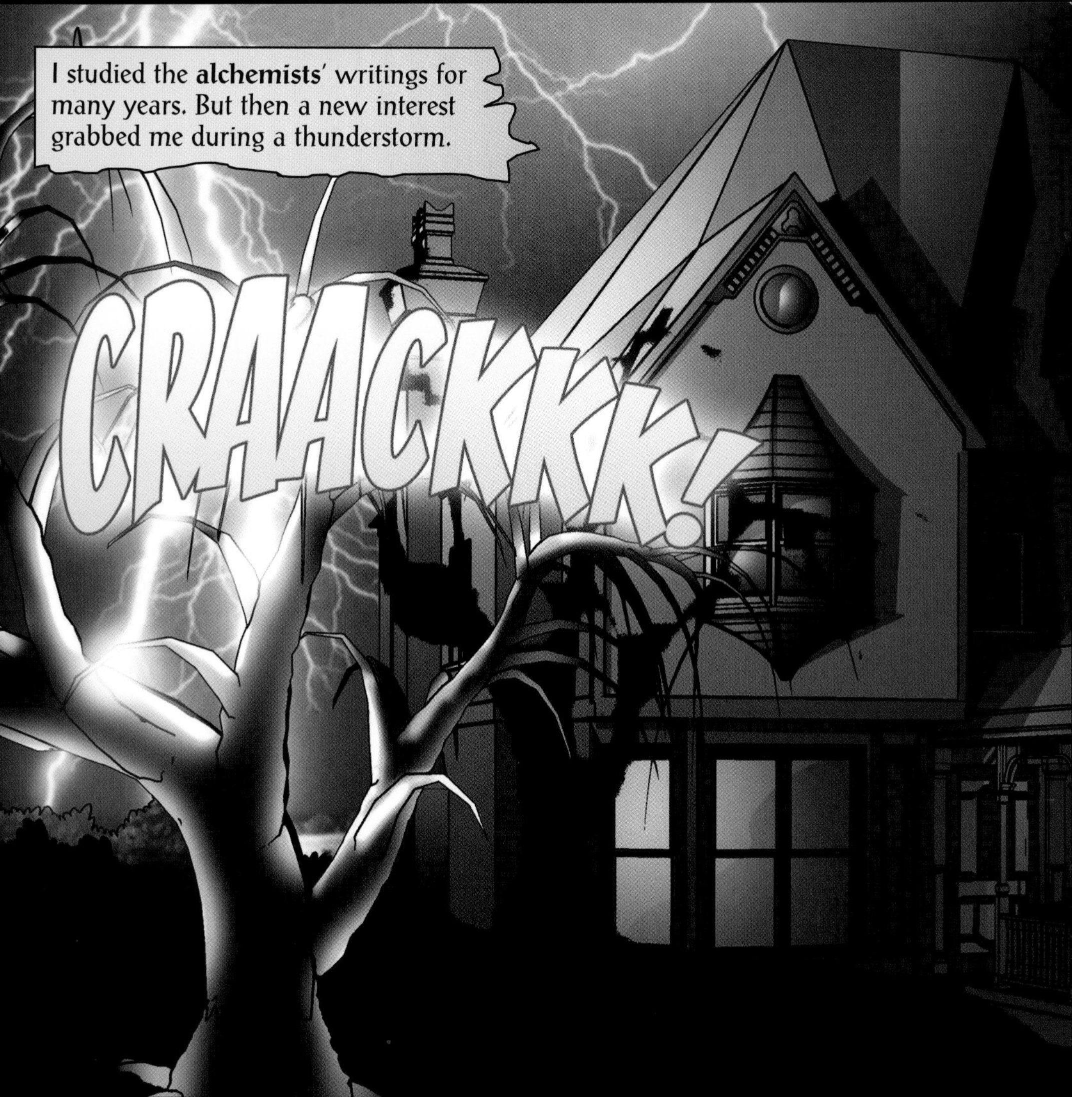
I studied the **alchemists**' writings for many years. But then a new interest grabbed me during a thunderstorm.
CRAACKKK!

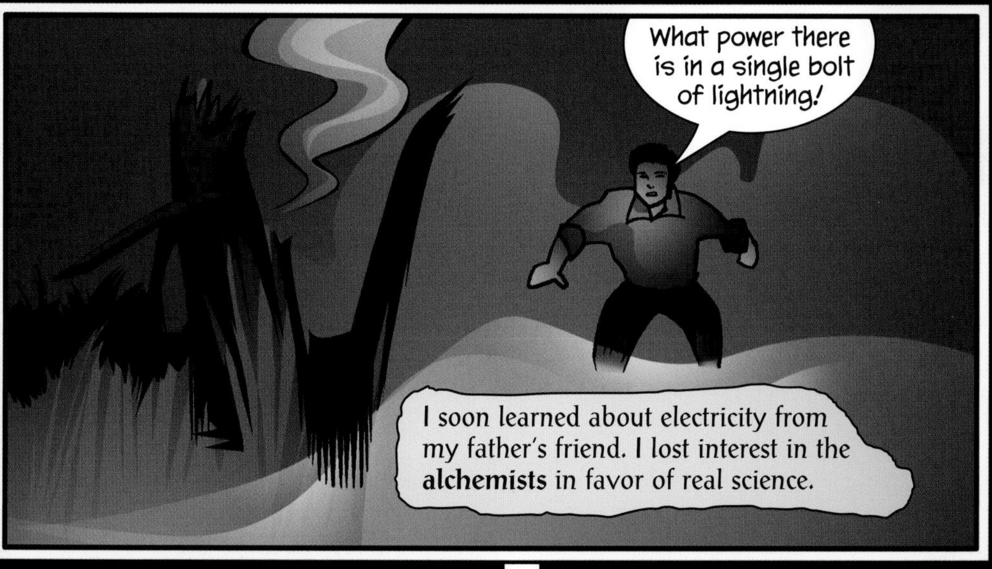
What power there is in a single bolt of lightning!
I soon learned about electricity from my father's friend. I lost interest in the **alchemists** in favor of real science.

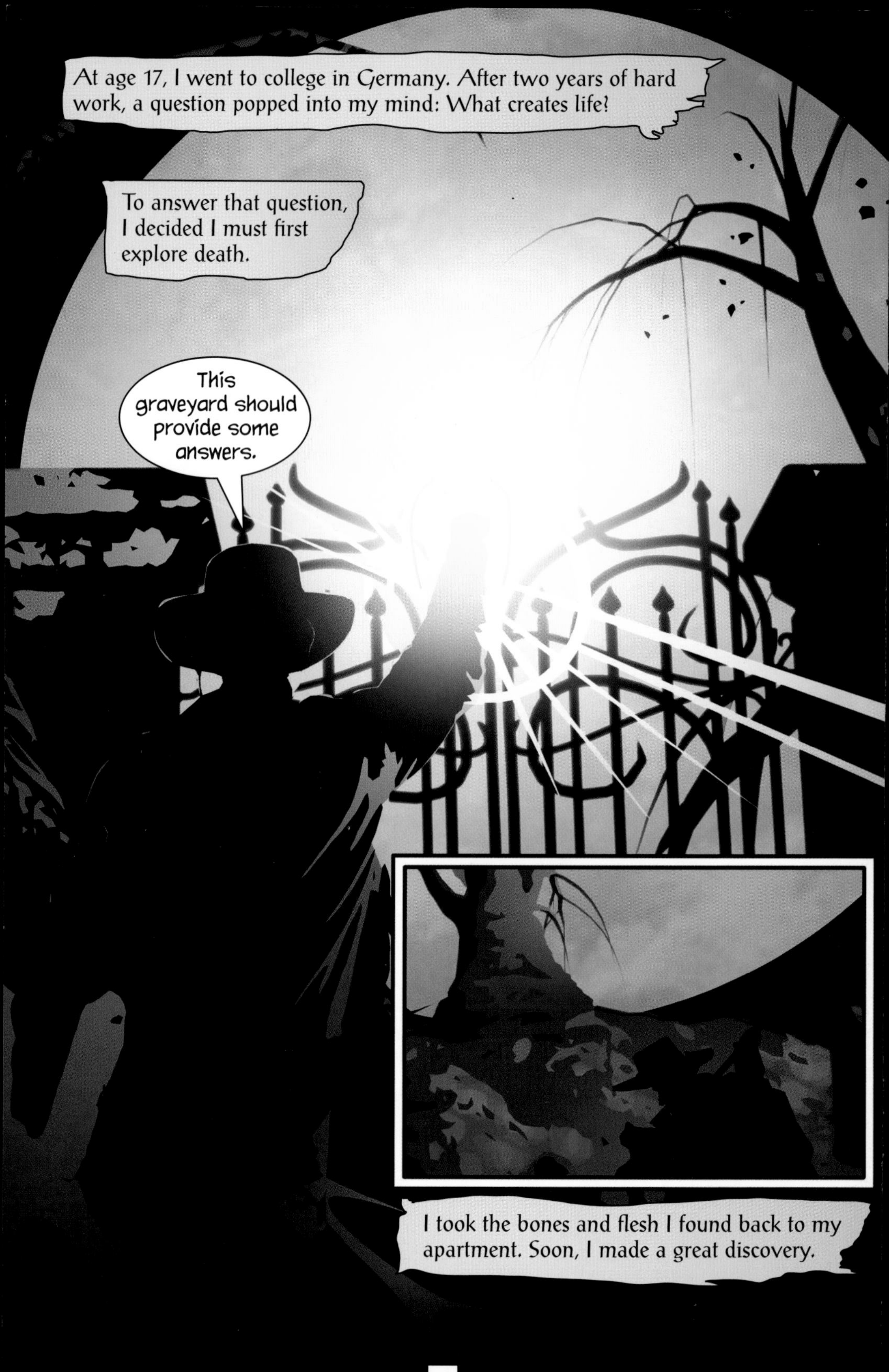
At age 17, I went to college in Germany. After two years of hard work, a question popped into my mind: What creates life?
To answer that question, I decided I must first explore death.
This graveyard should provide some answers.
I took the bones and flesh I found back to my apartment. Soon, I made a great discovery.

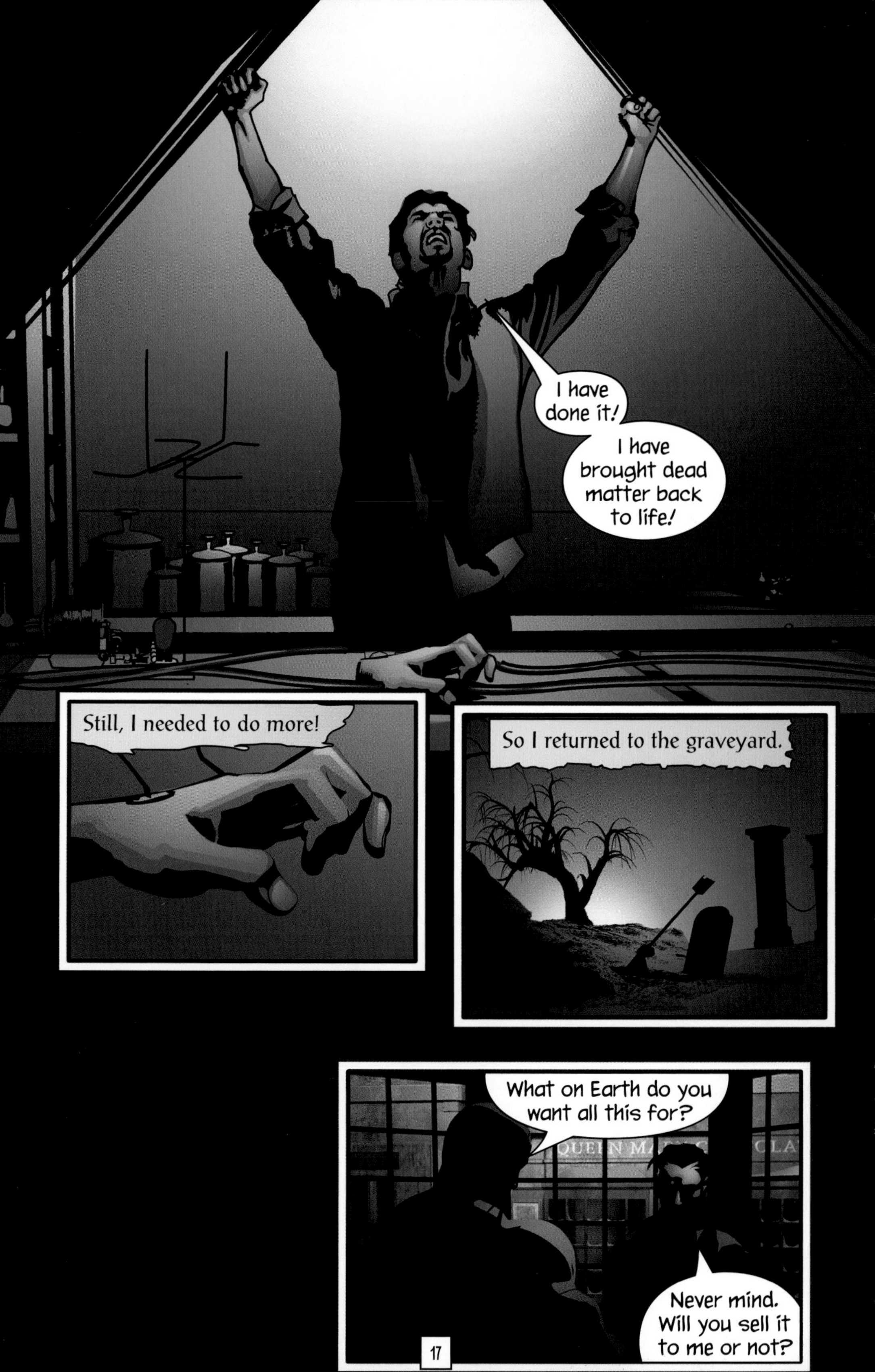
I have done it!
I have brought dead matter back to life!
Still, I needed to do more!
So I returned to the graveyard.
What on Earth do you want all this for?
Never mind. Will you sell it to me or not?

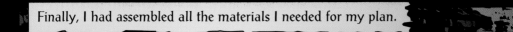

Finally, I had assembled all the materials I needed for my plan.

What are you doing in that apartment of yours?

None of your business.

He's a great scientist, too good for simple students like us.

From dead skin and bones, I would create a living being. Electricity would bring it to life. And my creature would treat me as if I were a god. The work, however, took time.

They make fun of me now. But wait until they see my creation!

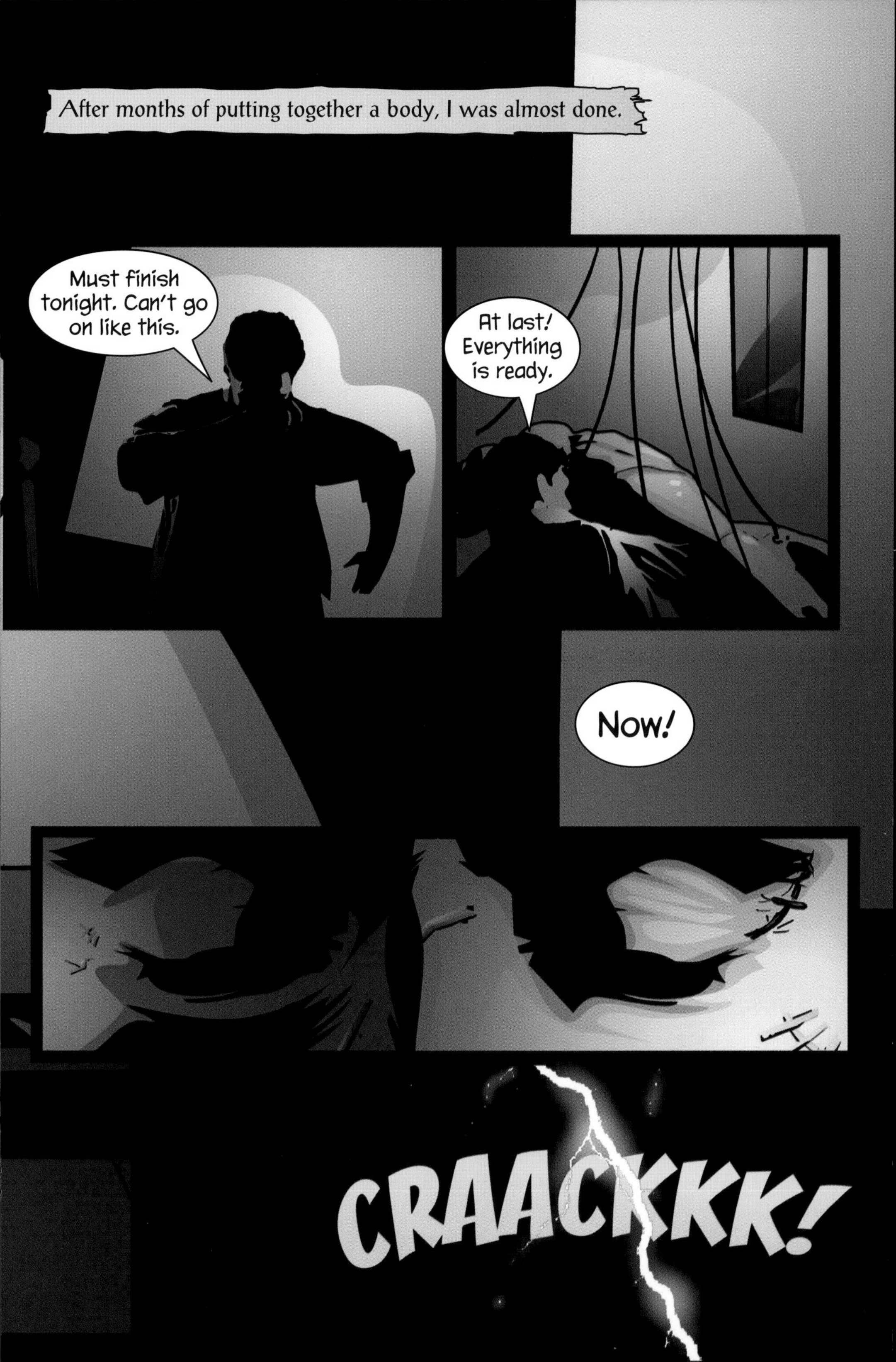
After months of putting together a body, I was almost done.
Must finish tonight. Can't go on like this.
At last! Everything is ready.
Now!
CRAACKKK!

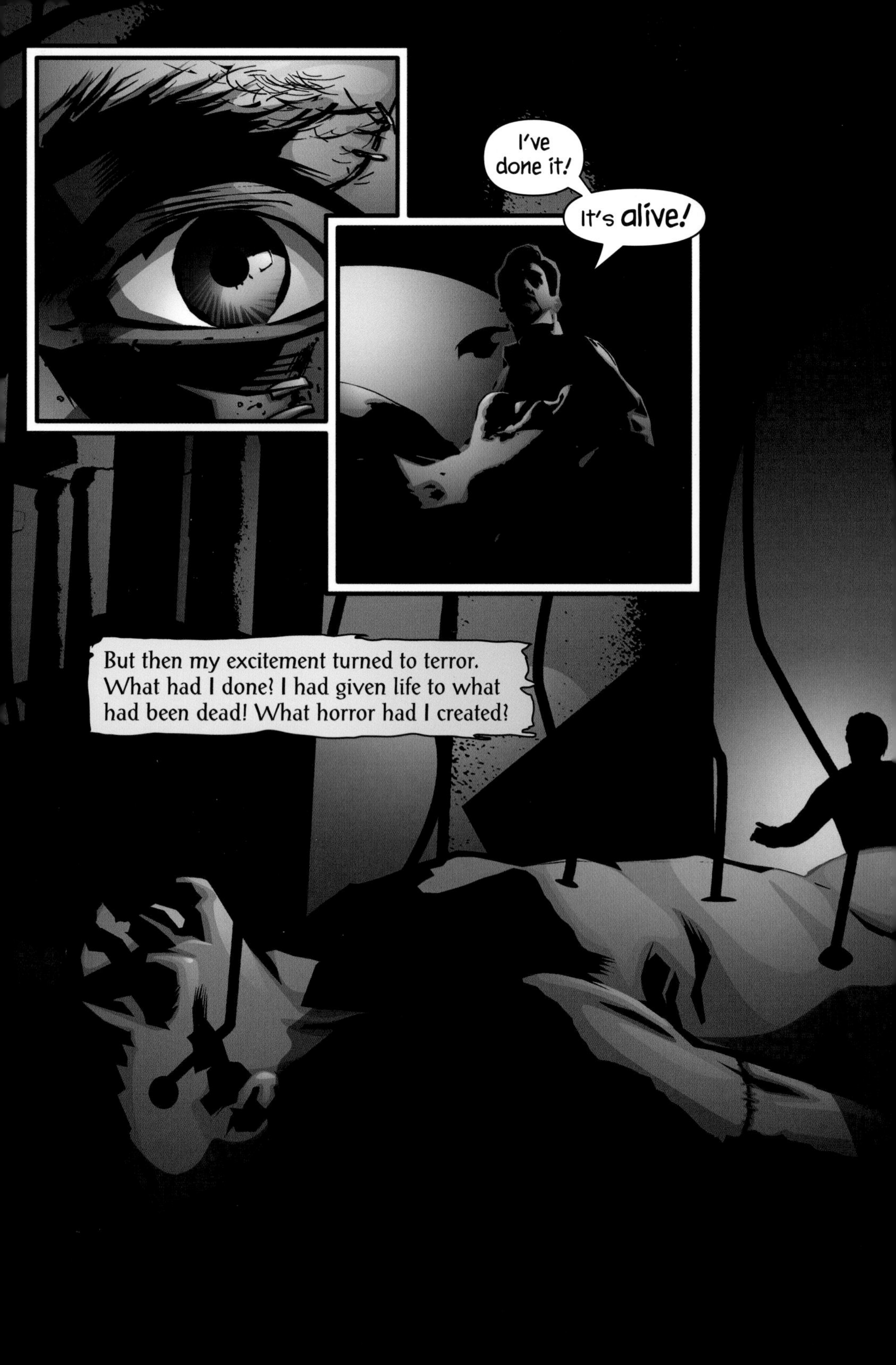
I've done it!
It's alive!
But then my excitement turned to terror. What had I done? I had given life to what had been dead! What horror had I created?

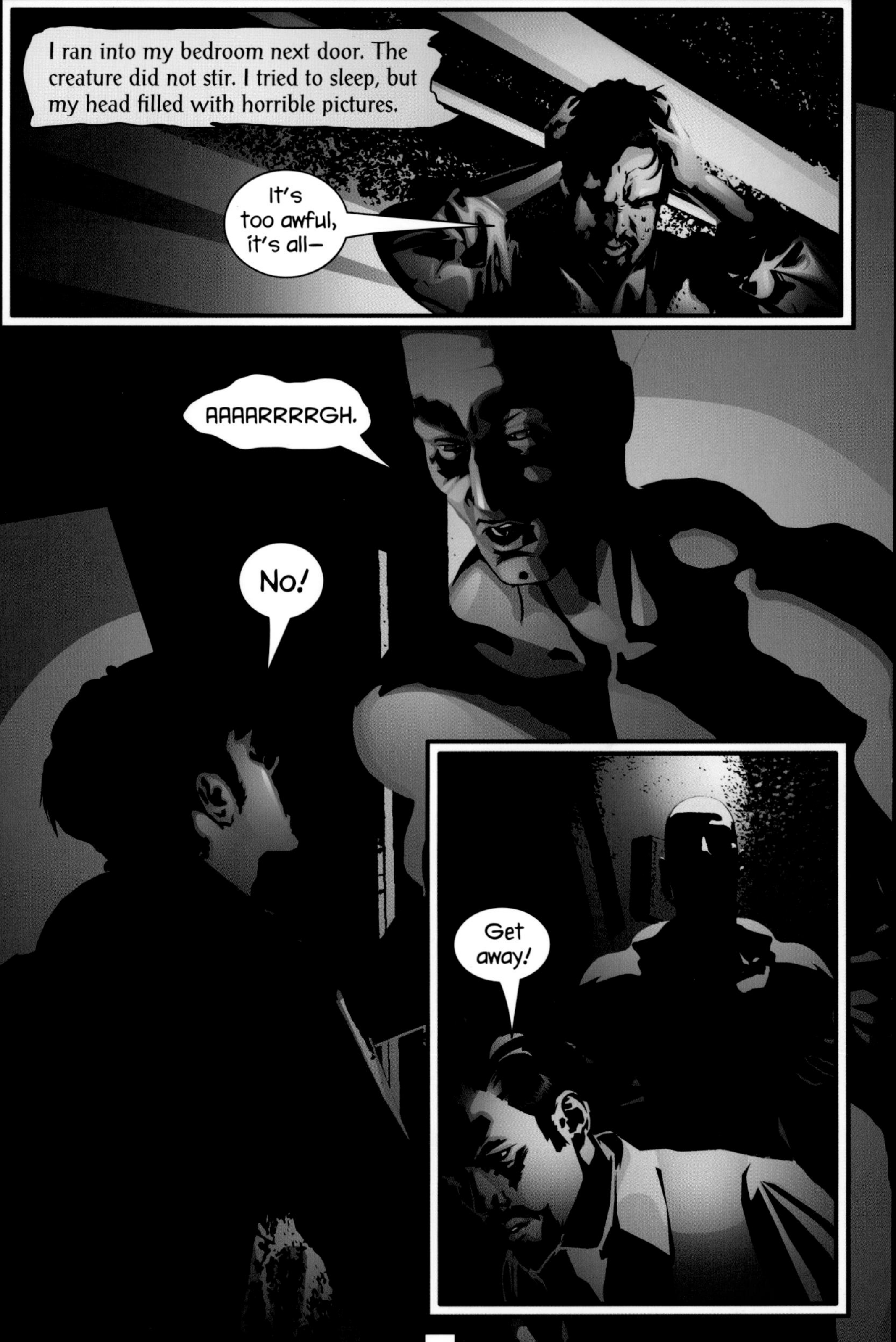
I ran into my bedroom next door. The creature did not stir. I tried to sleep, but my head filled with horrible pictures.
It's too awful, it's all—
AAAARRRRGH.
No!
Get away!

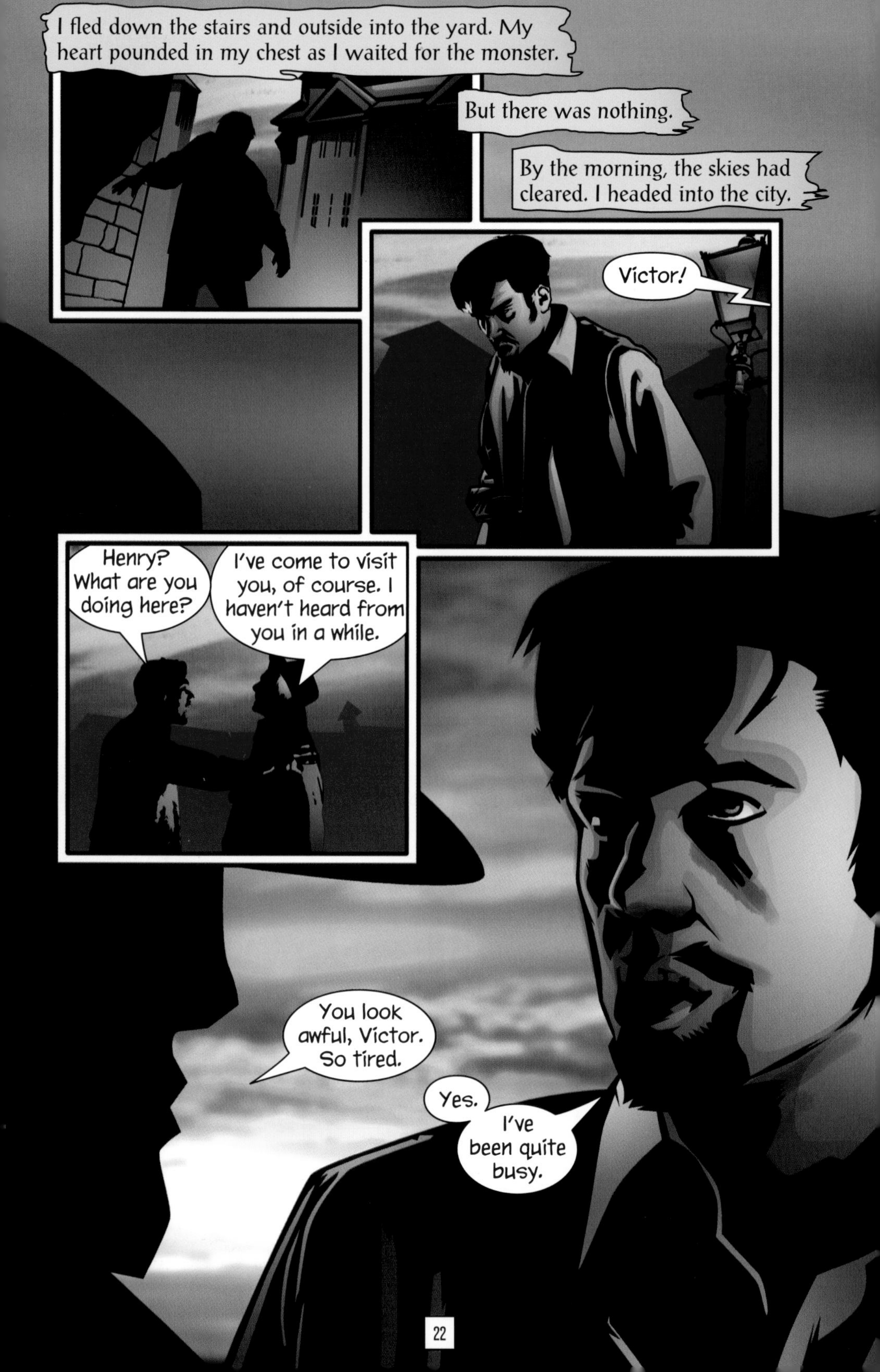
I fled down the stairs and outside into the yard. My heart pounded in my chest as I waited for the monster.
But there was nothing.
By the morning, the skies had cleared. I headed into the city.
Victor!
Henry? What are you doing here?
I've come to visit you, of course. I haven't heard from you in a while.
You look awful, Victor. So tired.
Yes.
I've been quite busy.

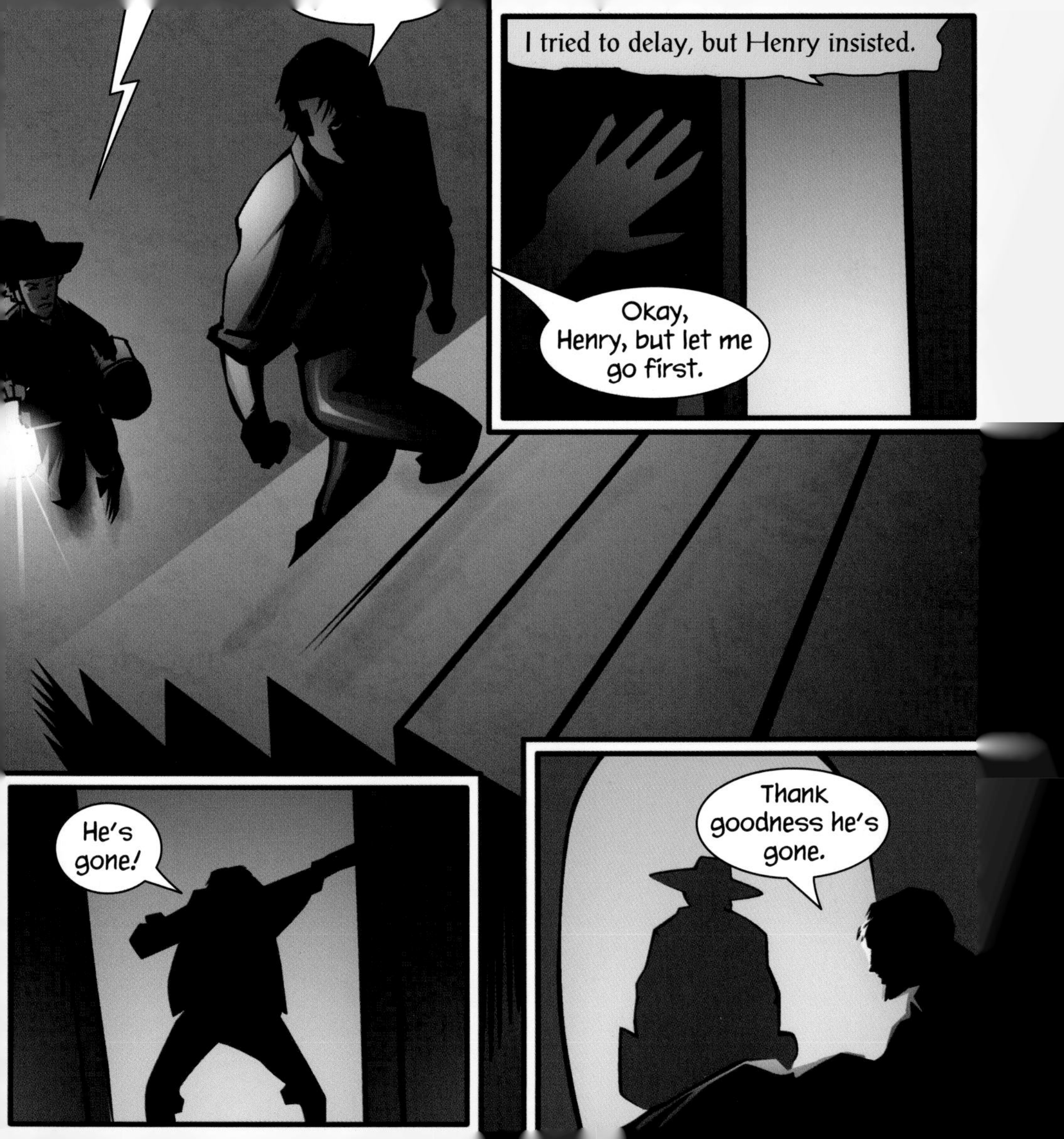
I tried to delay, but Henry insisted.
Okay, Henry, but let me go first.
He's gone!
Thank goodness he's gone.

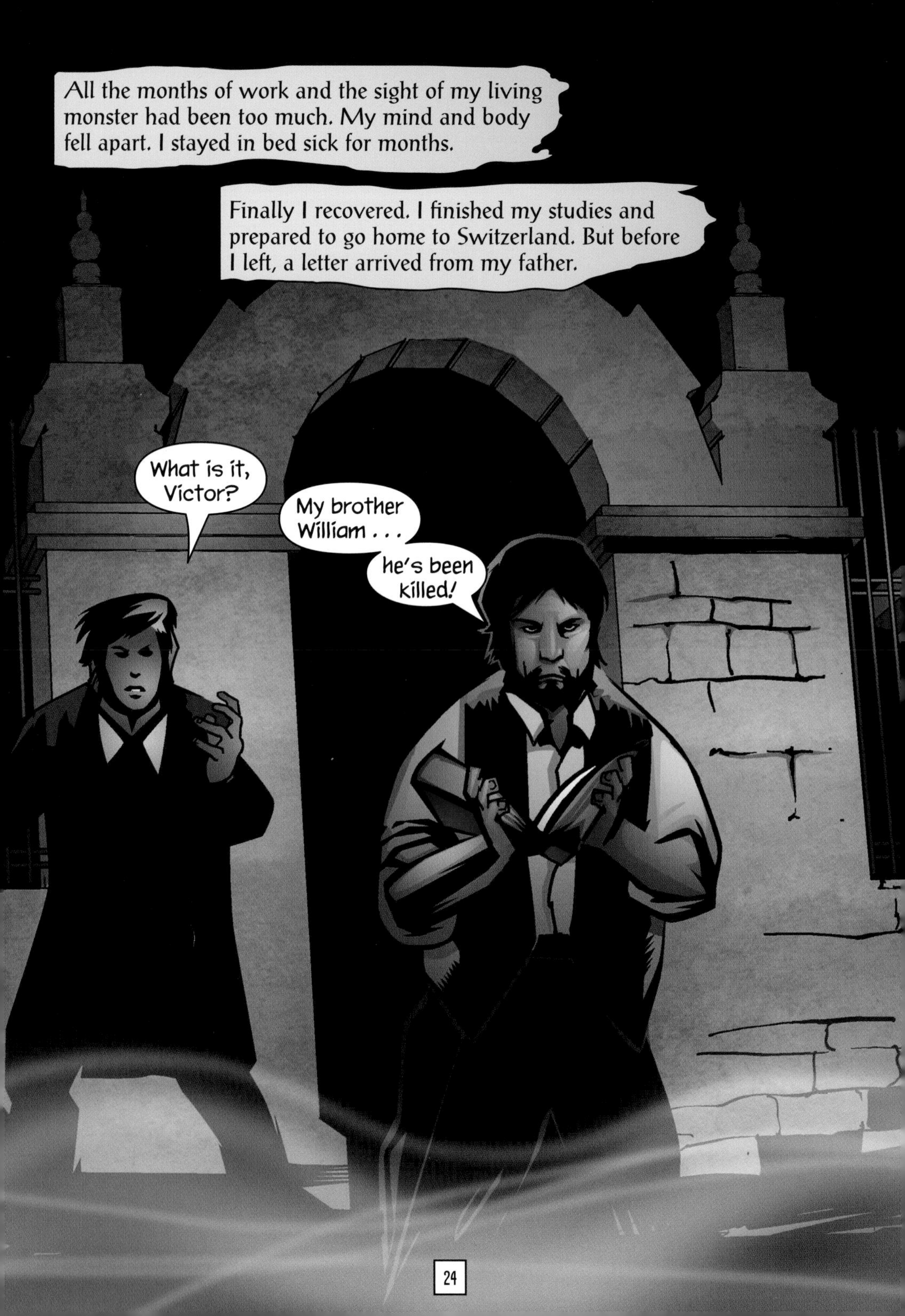
All the months of work and the sight of my living monster had been too much. My mind and body fell apart. I stayed in bed sick for months.
Finally I recovered. I finished my studies and prepared to go home to Switzerland. But before I left, a letter arrived from my father.
What is it, Victor?
My brother William . . .
he's been killed!

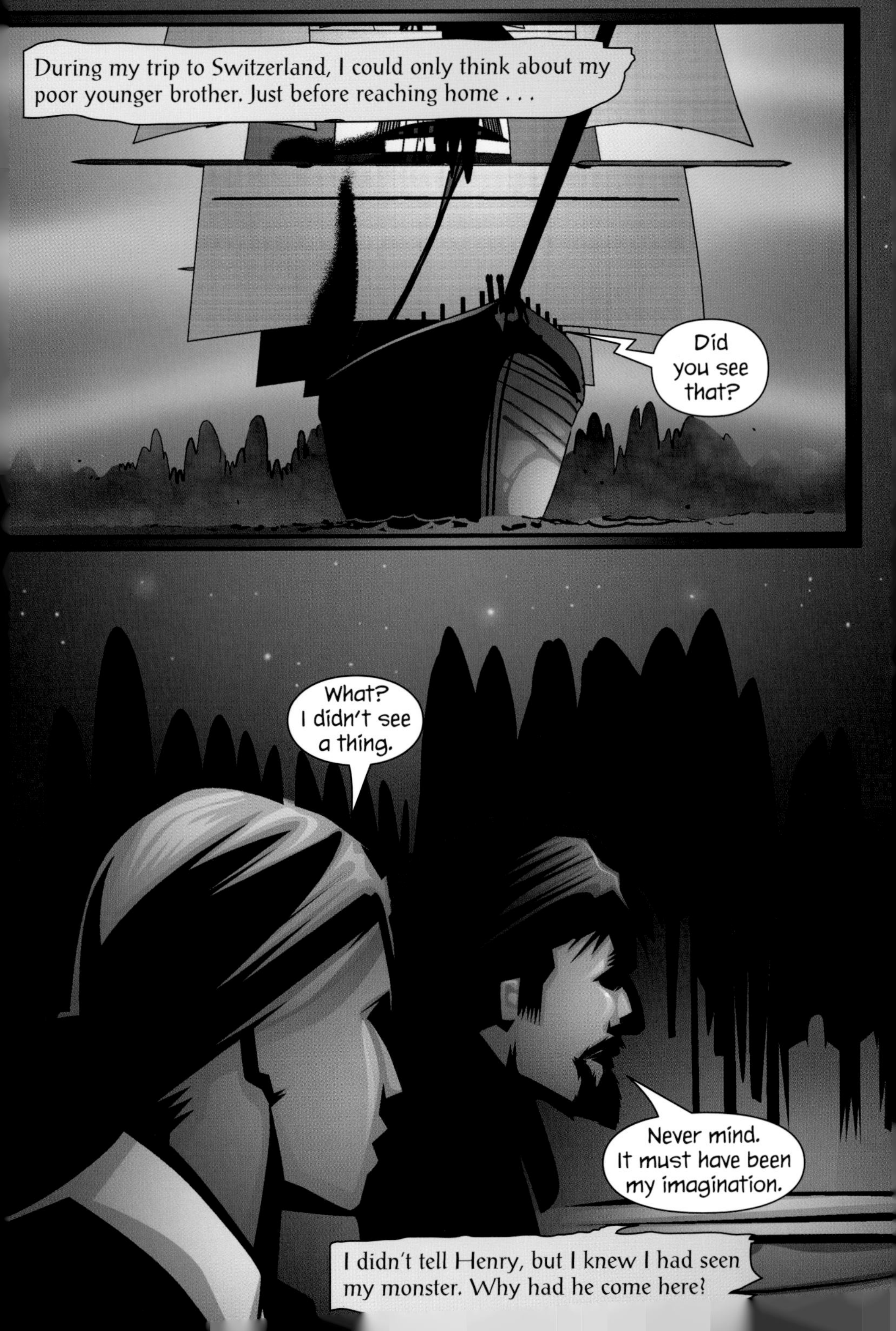

During my trip to Switzerland, I could only think about my poor younger brother. Just before reaching home . . .
Did you see that?
What? I didn't see a thing.
Never mind. It must have been my imagination.
I didn't tell Henry, but I knew I had seen my monster. Why had he come here?

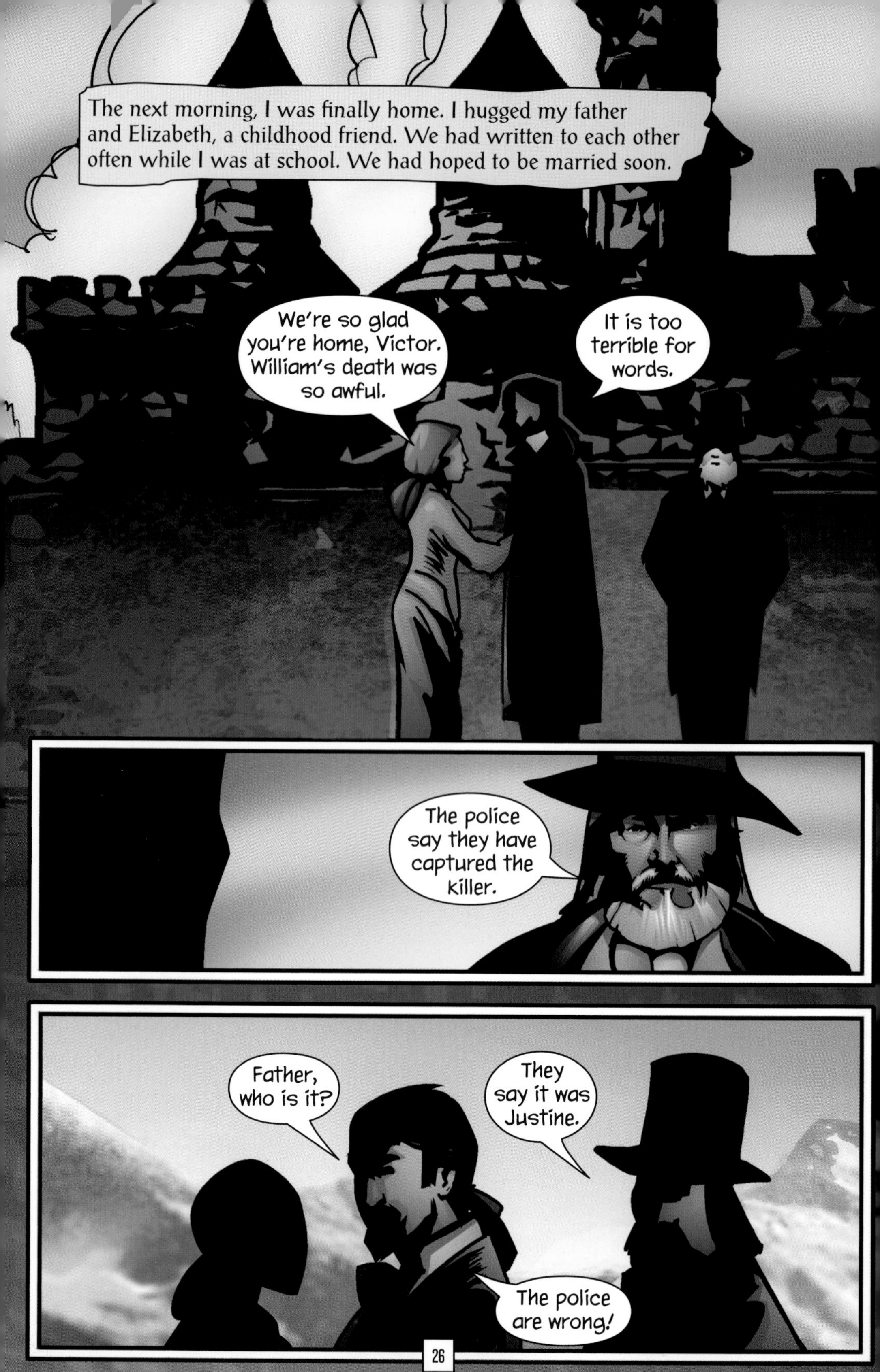
The next morning, I was finally home. I hugged my father and Elizabeth, a childhood friend. We had written to each other often while I was at school. We had hoped to be married soon.
We're so glad you're home, Victor. William's death was so awful.
It is too terrible for words.
The police say they have captured the killer.
Father, who is it?
They say it was Justine.
The police are wrong!

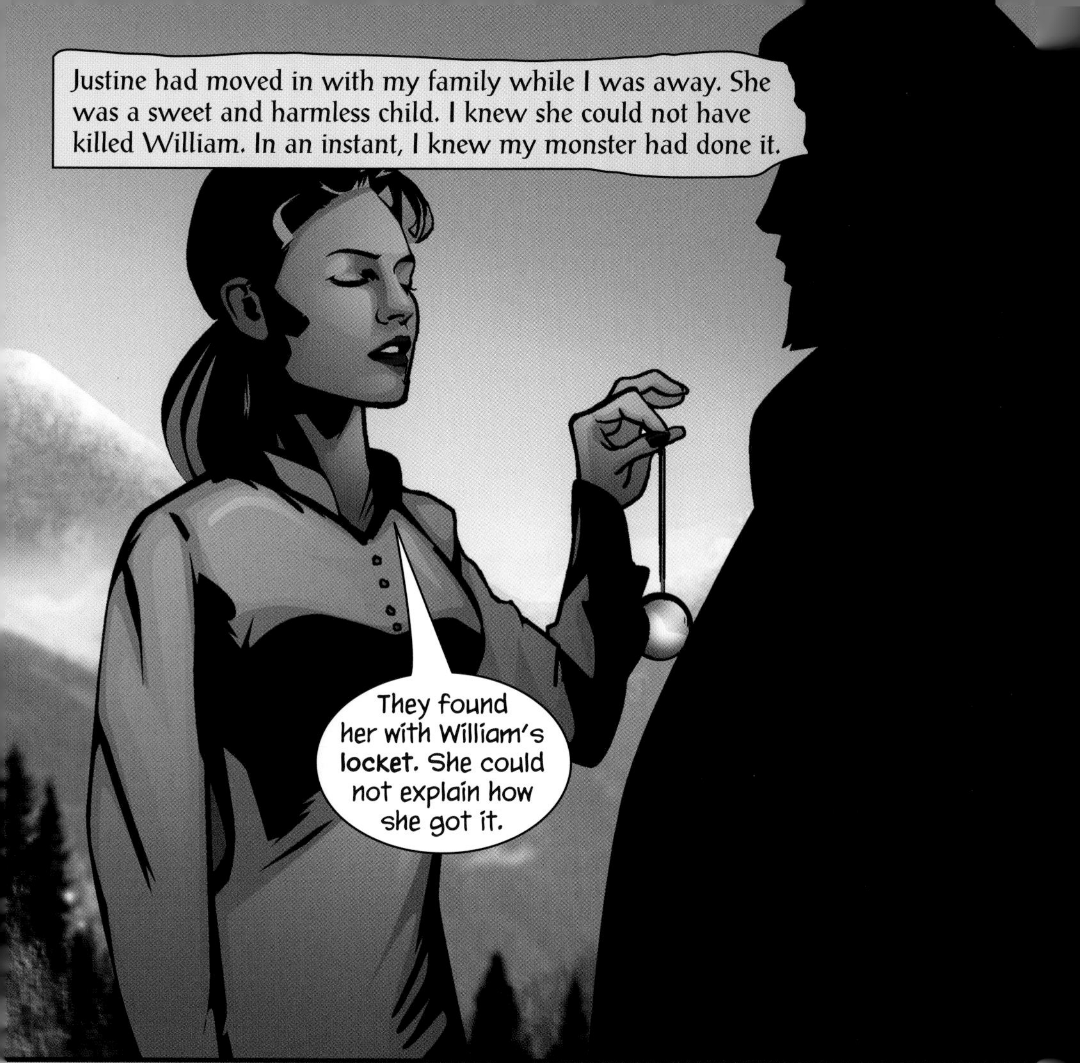
Justine had moved in with my family while I was away. She was a sweet and harmless child. I knew she could not have killed William. In an instant, I knew my monster had done it.
They found her with William's locket. She could not explain how she got it.

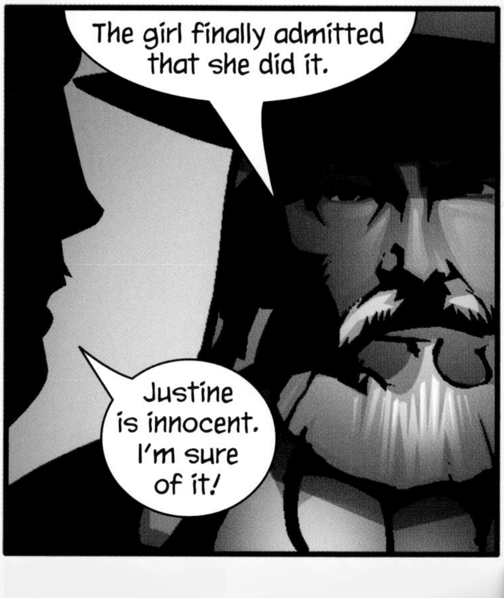
The girl finally admitted that she did it.
Justine is innocent. I'm sure of it!

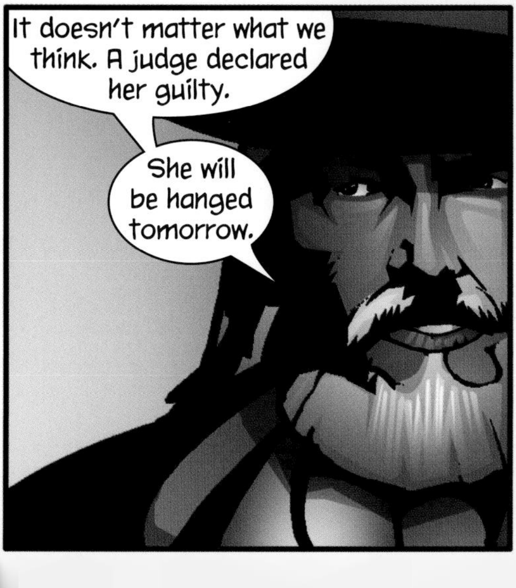
It doesn't matter what we think. A judge declared her guilty.
She will be hanged tomorrow.

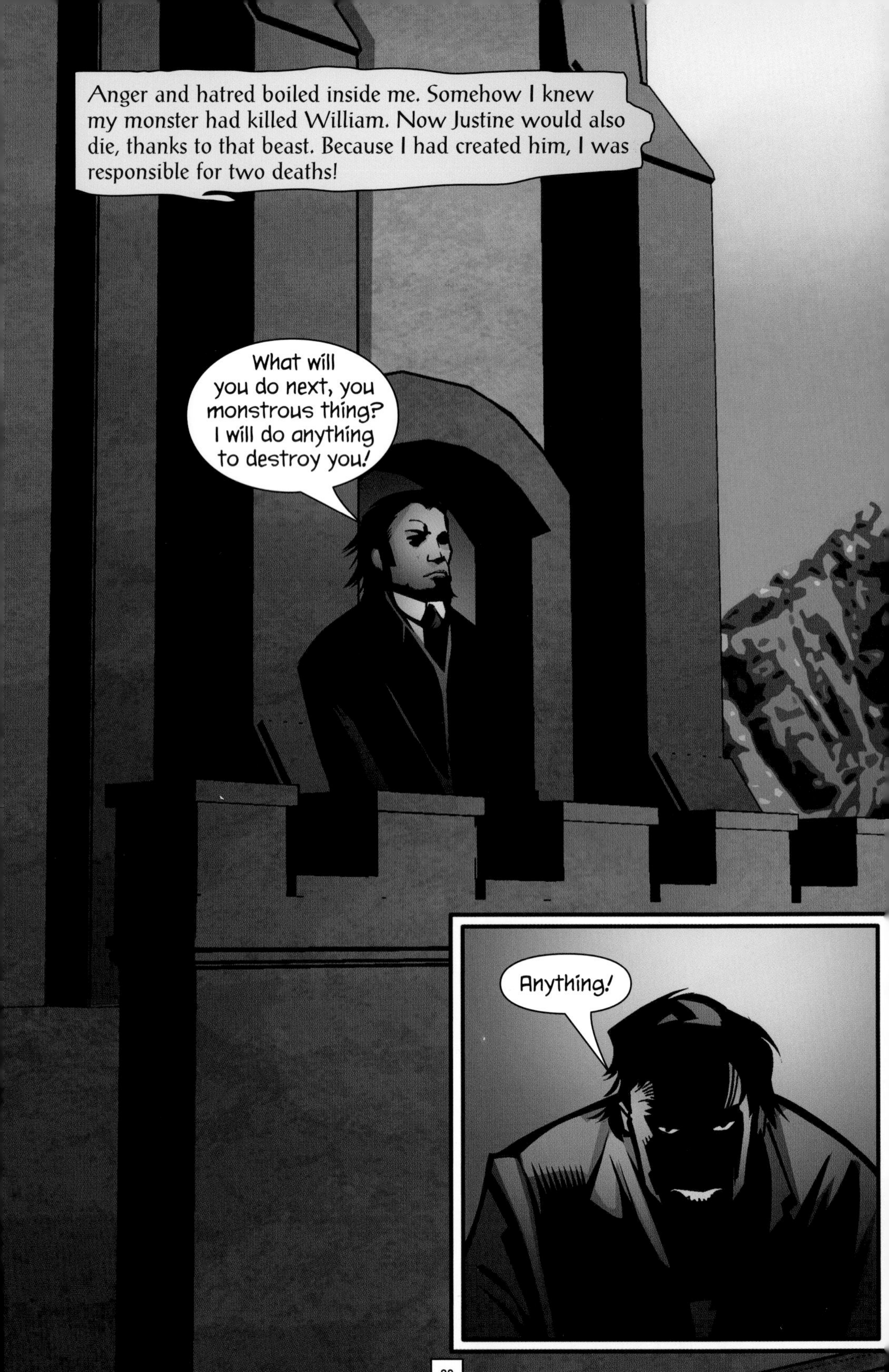
Anger and hatred boiled inside me. Somehow I knew my monster had killed William. Now Justine would also die, thanks to that beast. Because I had created him, I was responsible for two deaths!
What will you do next, you monstrous thing? I will do anything to destroy you!
Anything!

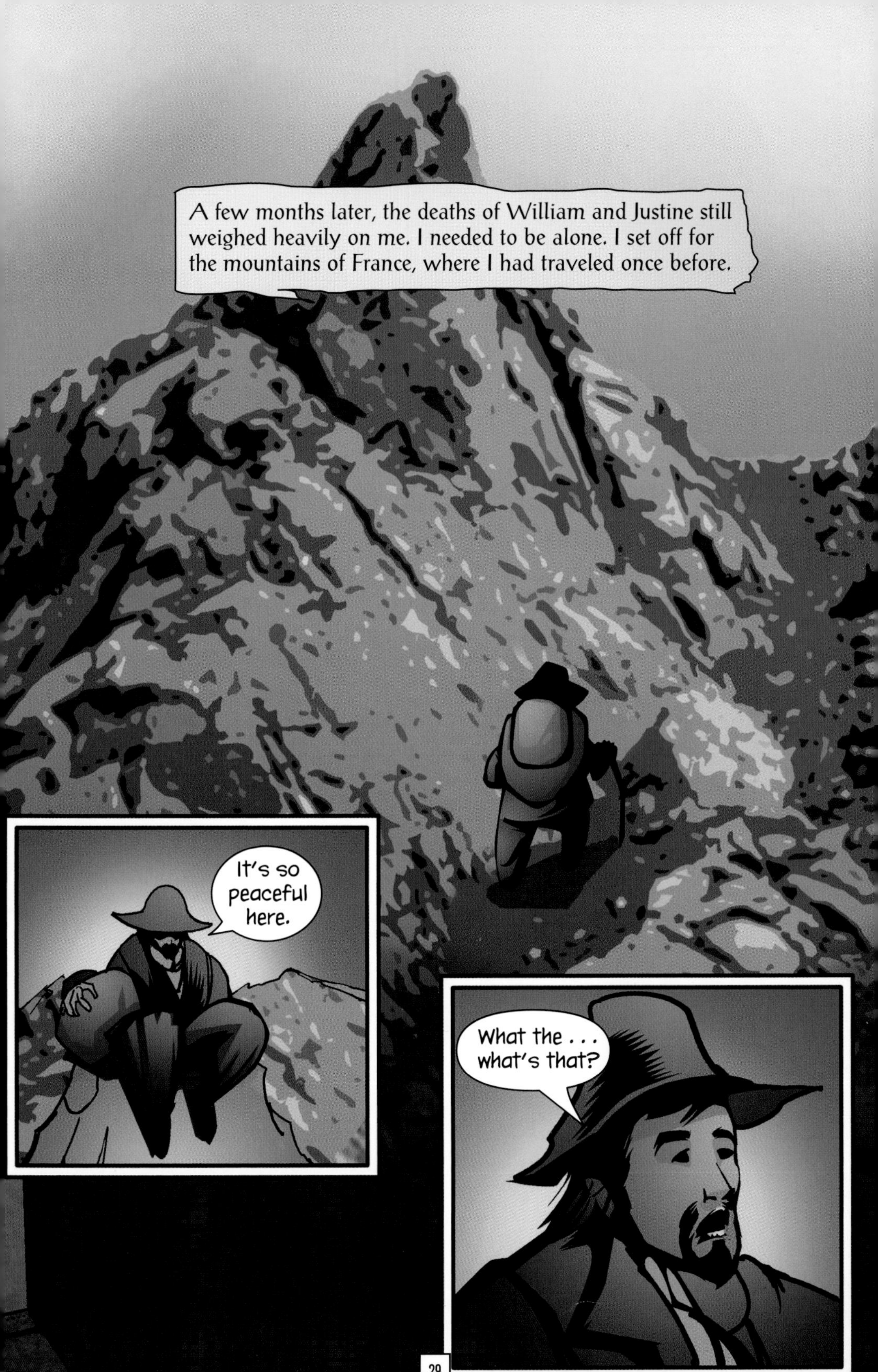
A few months later, the deaths of William and Justine still weighed heavily on me. I needed to be alone. I set off for the mountains of France, where I had traveled once before.
It's so peaceful here.
What the . . . what's that?

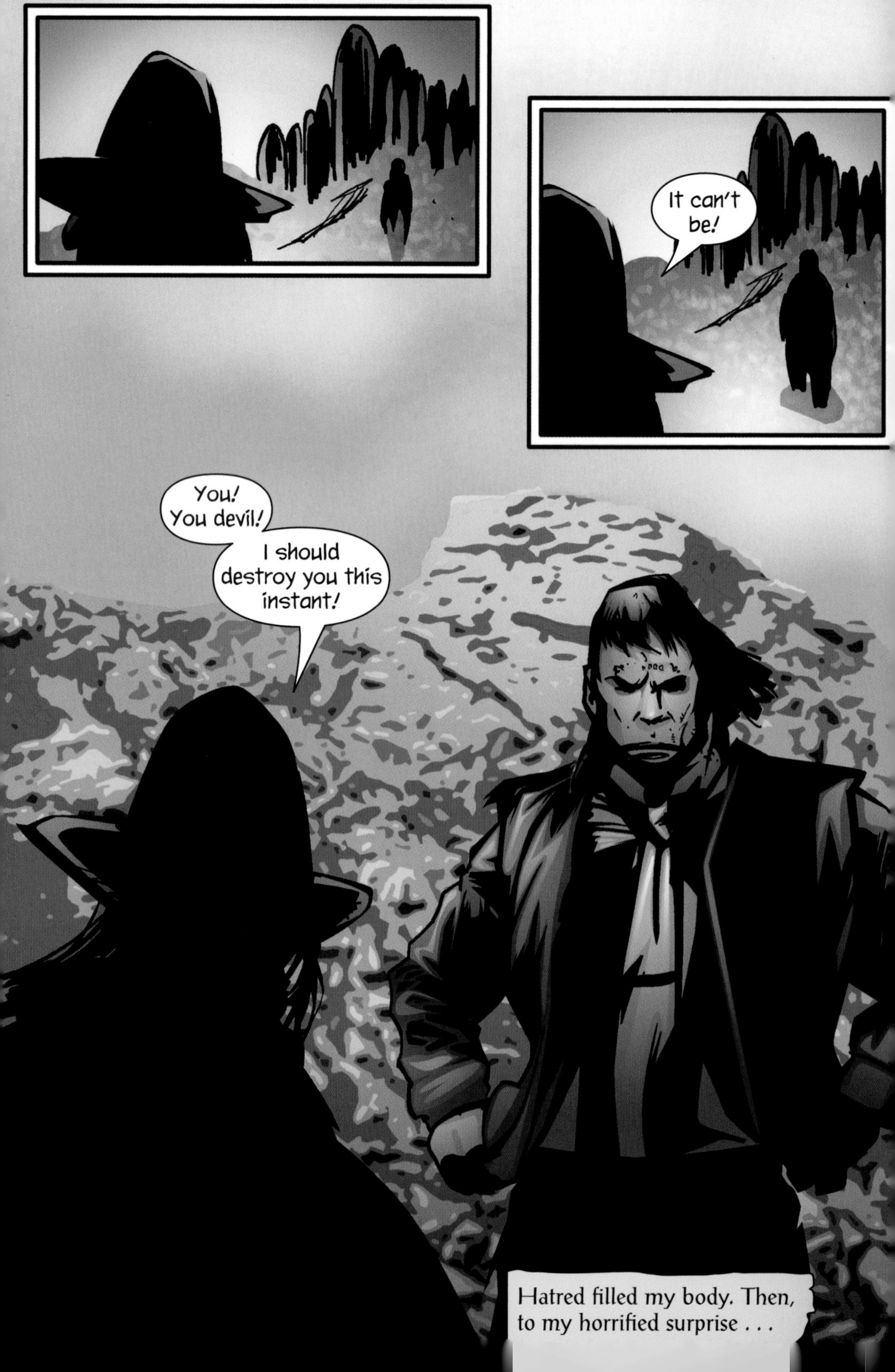
It can't be!
You! You devil!
I should destroy you this instant!
Hatred filled my body. Then, to my horrified surprise . . .

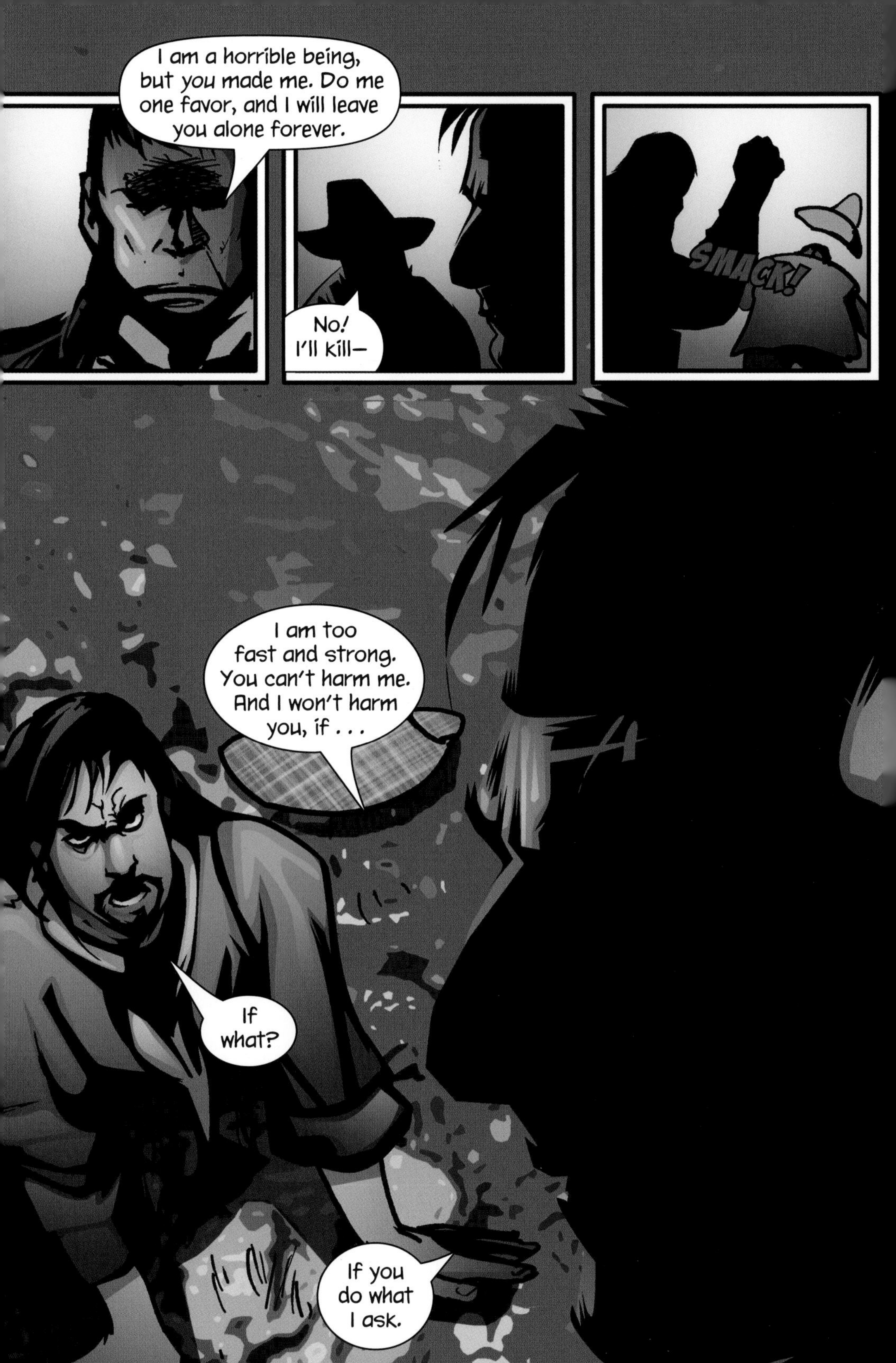
I am a horrible being, but you made me. Do me one favor, and I will leave you alone forever.
No! I'll kill—
SMACK!
I am too fast and strong. You can't harm me. And I won't harm you, if . . .
If what?
If you do what I ask.

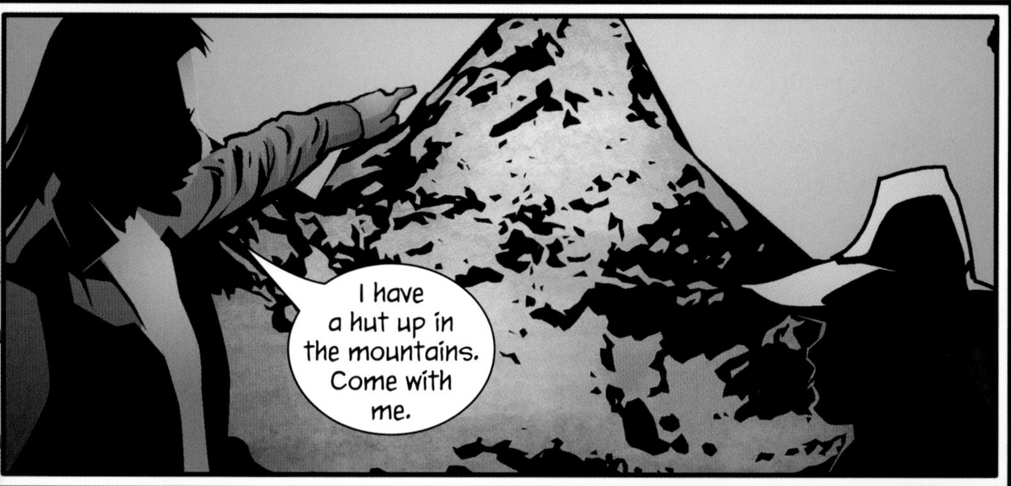
I have a hut up in the mountains. Come with me.

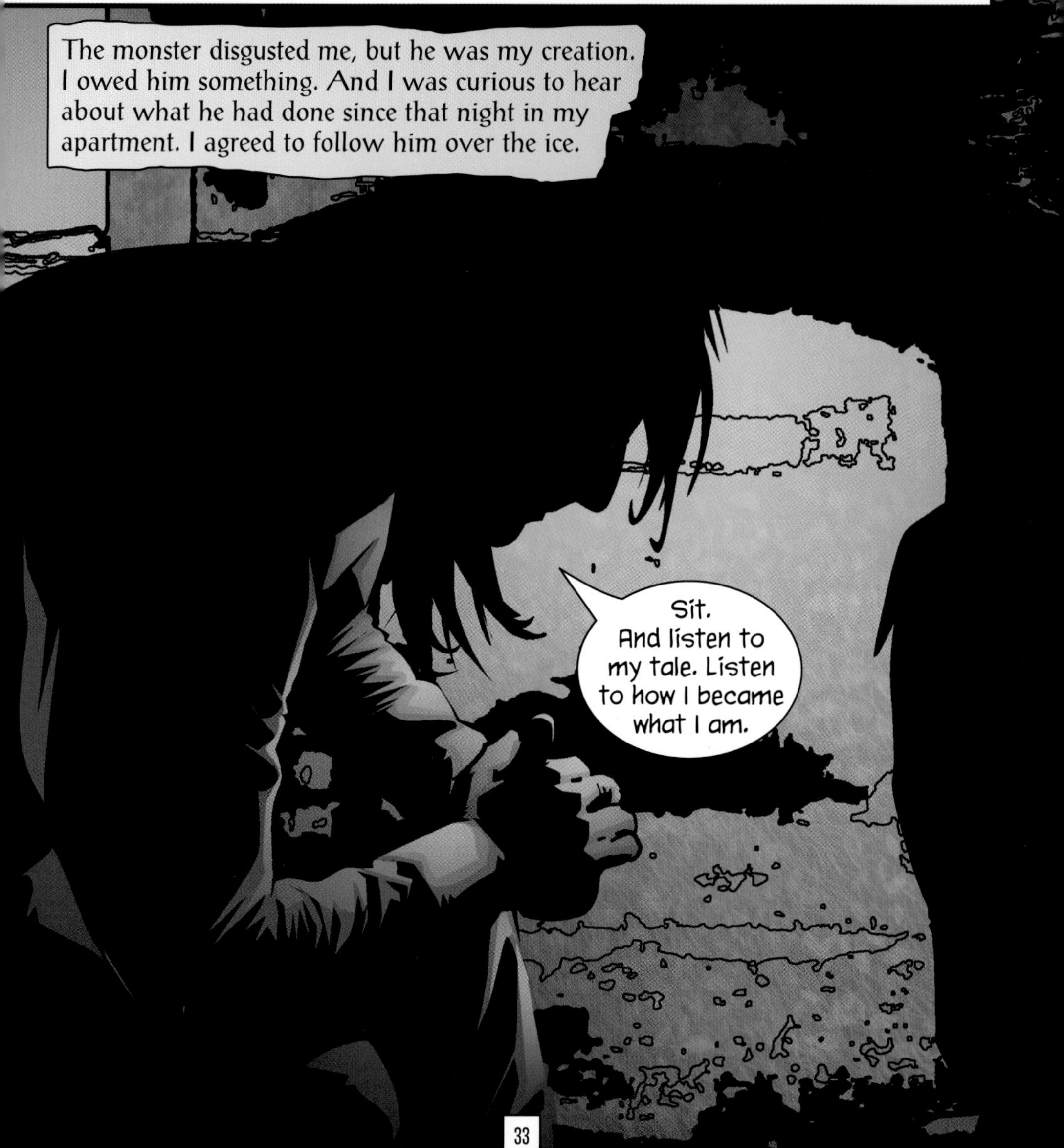
The monster disgusted me, but he was my creation. I owed him something. And I was curious to hear about what he had done since that night in my apartment. I agreed to follow him over the ice.
Sit. And listen to my tale. Listen to how I became what I am.

Before I left your apartment, I took some of your clothes. Then I went into the woods. I was like a newborn baby. I could move, but I knew nothing about the world. I looked for food to eat. I slept outside in the cold and the rain.
Then one day, I came to a **cottage** in a small village.
Ahhh! Mommy, help!
Get away! Get away from my children!

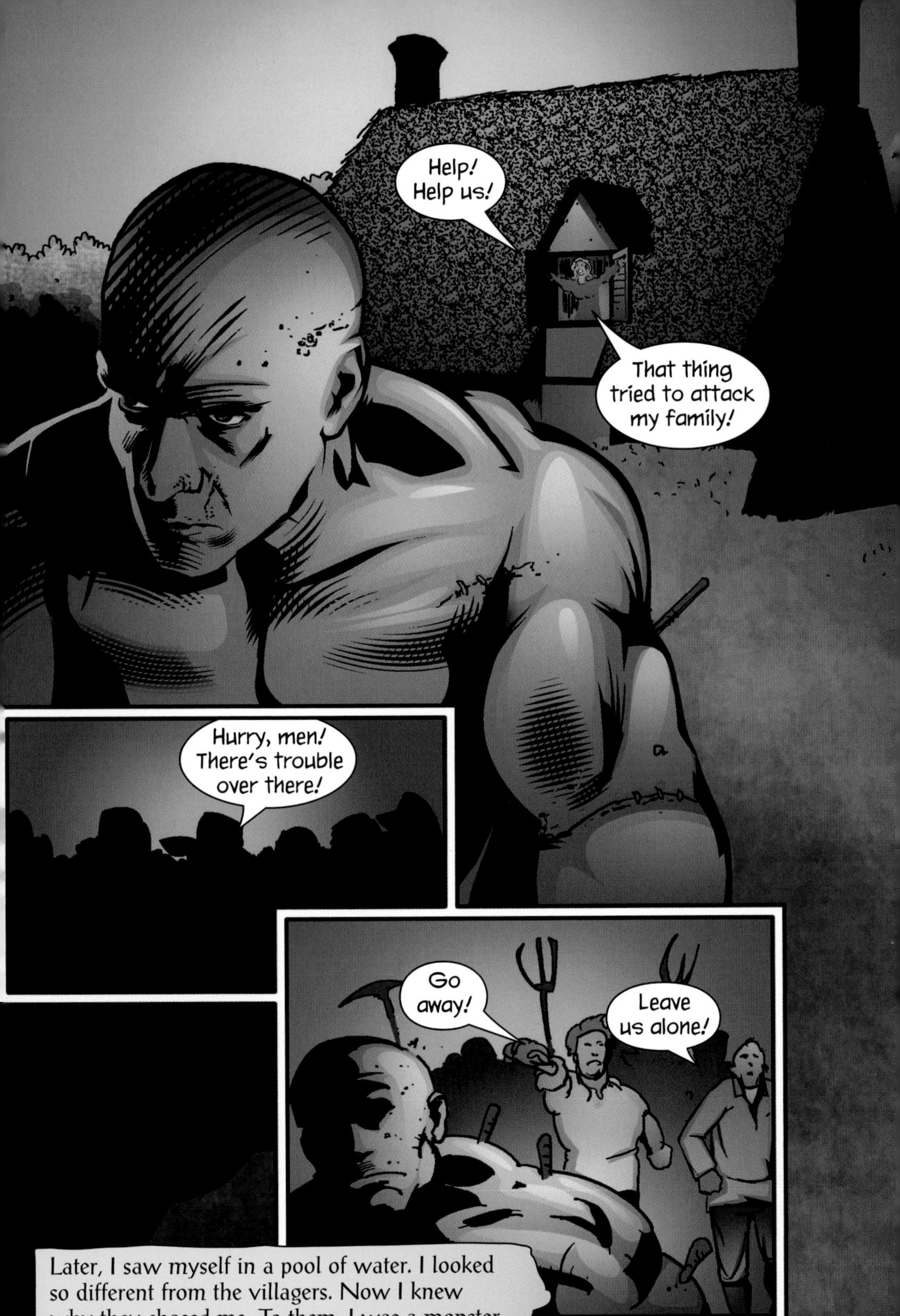
Help! Help us!
That thing tried to attack my family!
Hurry, men! There's trouble over there!
Go away!
Leave us alone!
Later, I saw myself in a pool of water. I looked so different from the villagers. Now I knew why they chased me. To them, I was a monster.

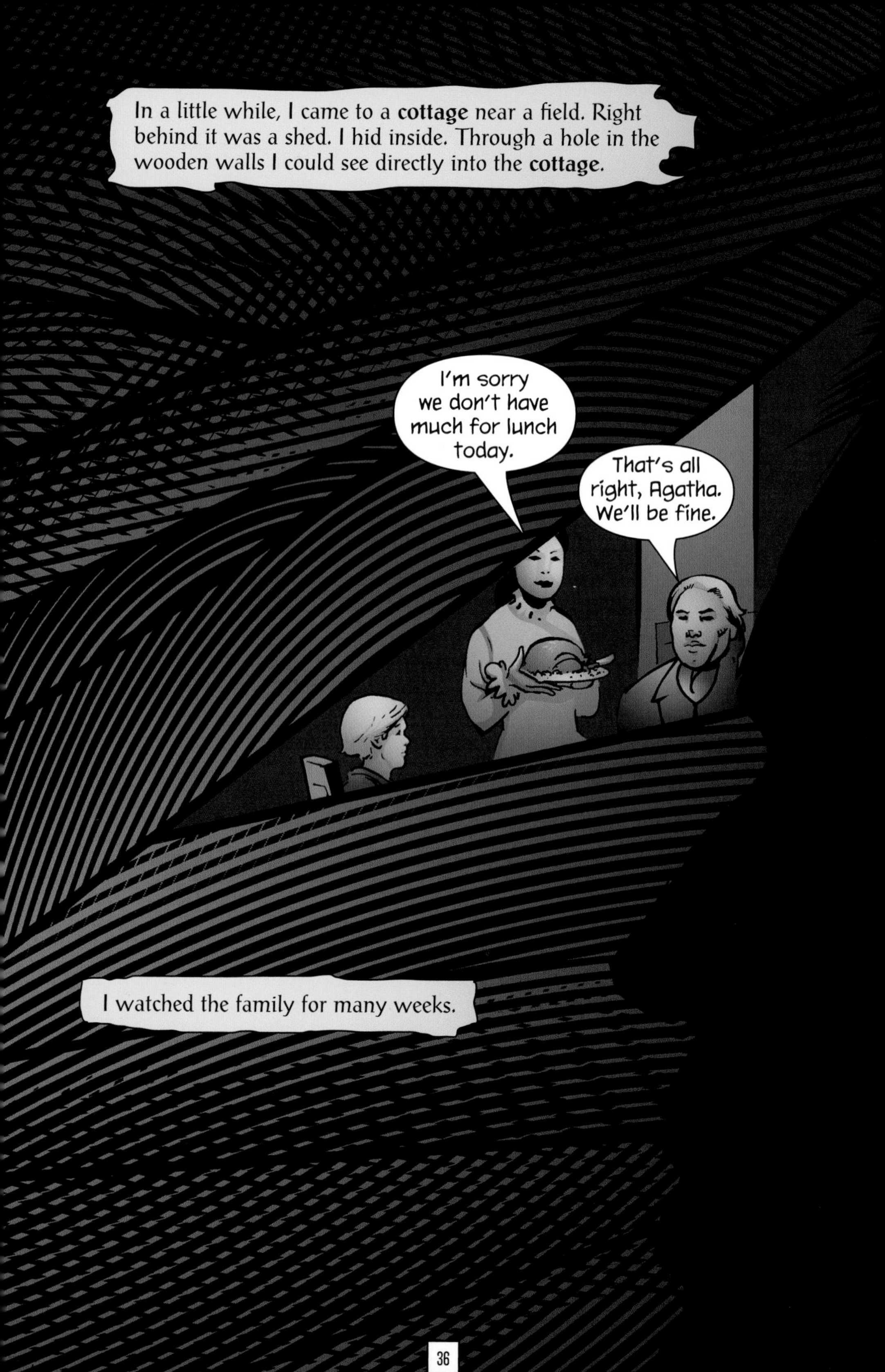
In a little while, I came to a **cottage** near a field. Right behind it was a shed. I hid inside. Through a hole in the wooden walls I could see directly into the **cottage**.
I'm sorry we don't have much for lunch today.
That's all right, Agatha. We'll be fine.
I watched the family for many weeks.

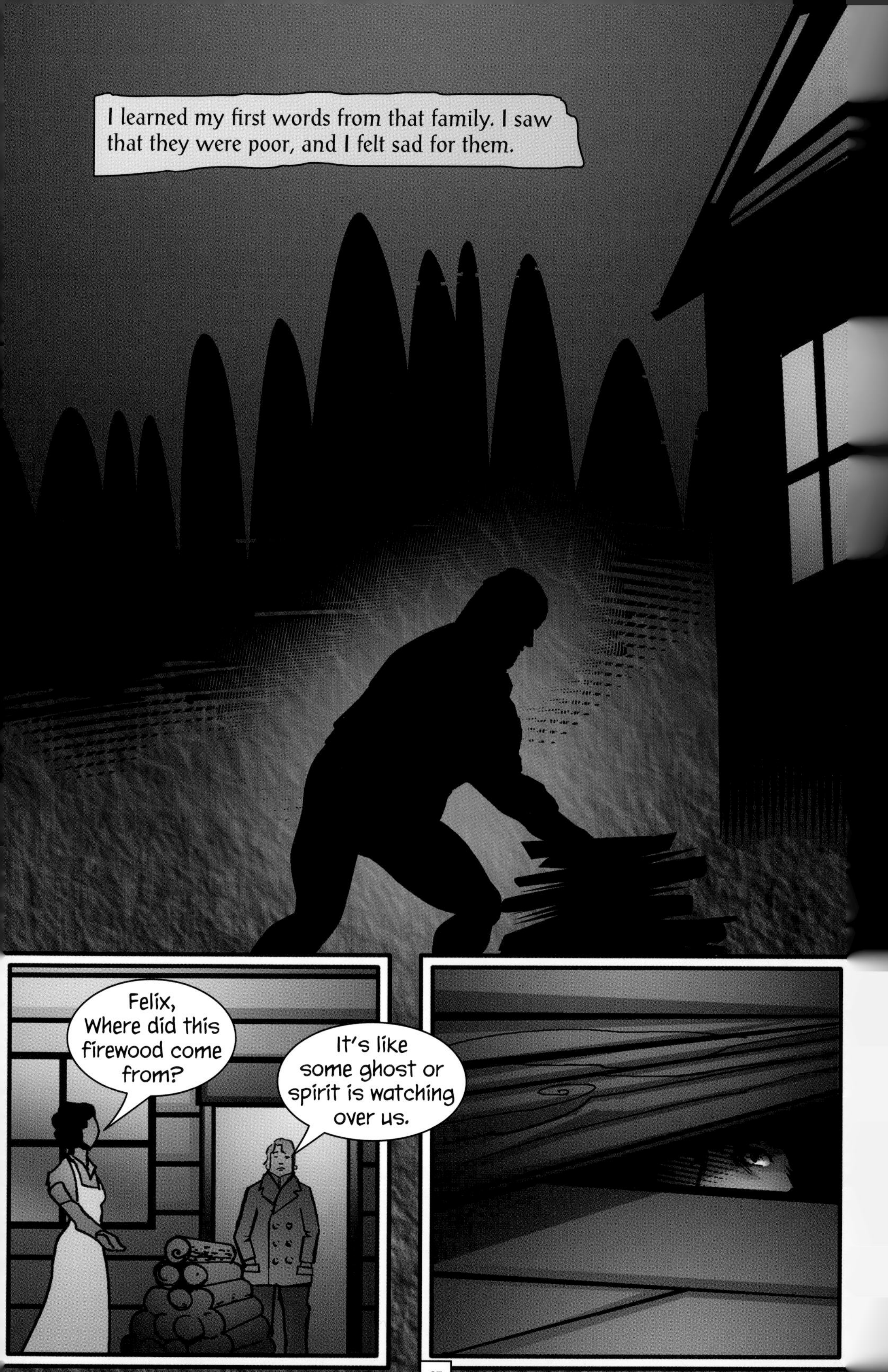
I learned my first words from that family. I saw that they were poor, and I felt sad for them.
Felix, Where did this firewood come from?
It's like some ghost or spirit is watching over us.

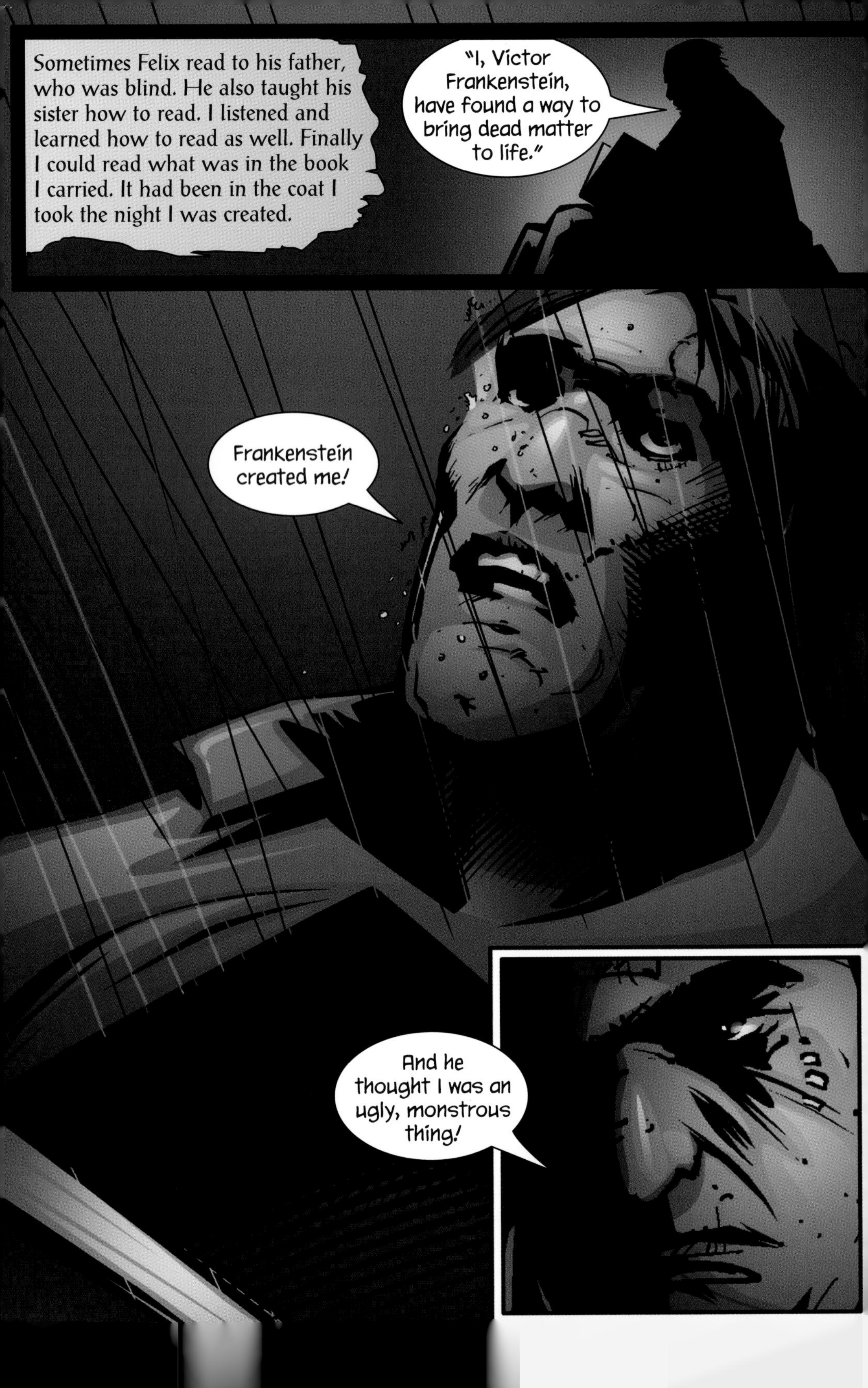
Sometimes Felix read to his father, who was blind. He also taught his sister how to read. I listened and learned how to read as well. Finally I could read what was in the book I carried. It had been in the coat I took the night I was created.
"I, Victor Frankenstein, have found a way to bring dead matter to life."
Frankenstein created me!
And he thought I was an ugly, monstrous thing!

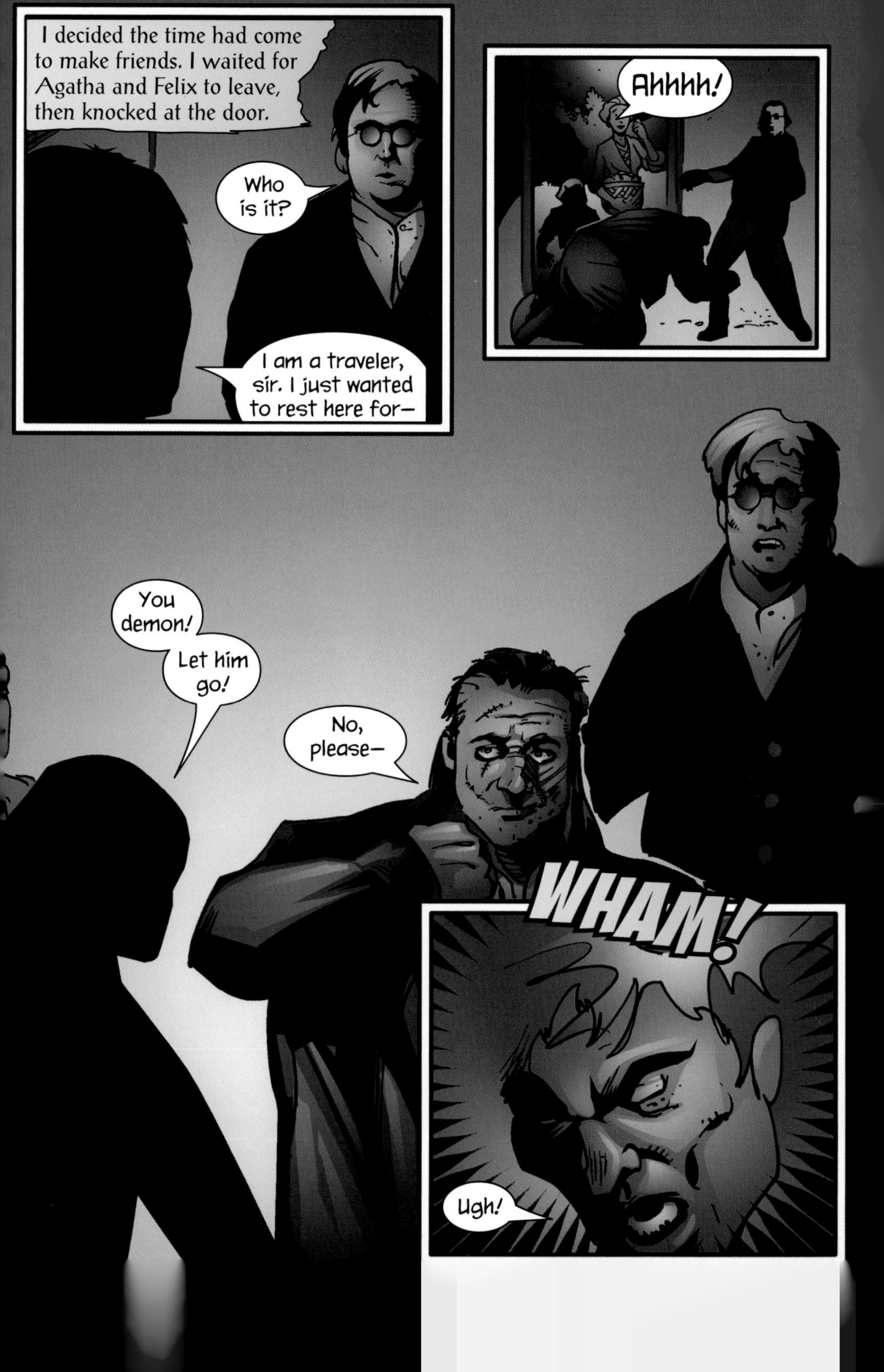
I decided the time had come to make friends. I waited for Agatha and Felix to leave, then knocked at the door.
Who is it?
I am a traveler, sir. I just wanted to rest here for—
Ahhhh!
You demon!
Let him go!
No, please—
WHAM!
Ugh!

I could have crushed the boy with one hand. Instead, I ran off into the woods.
You monster! Leave us alone!
I knew from your journal, Frankenstein, where you lived. I decided to track you down. Only you could end my suffering.

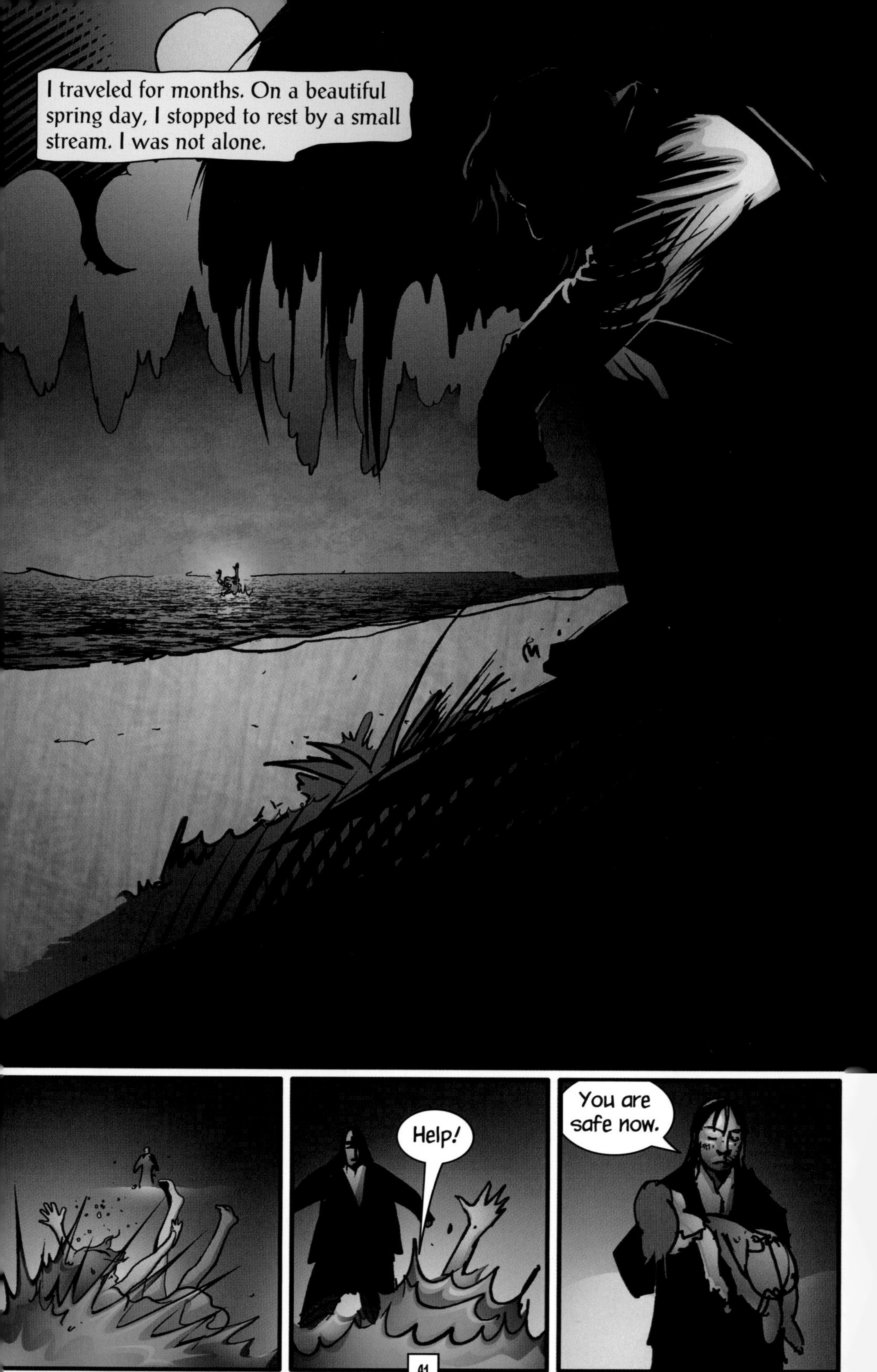

I traveled for months. On a beautiful spring day, I stopped to rest by a small stream. I was not alone.

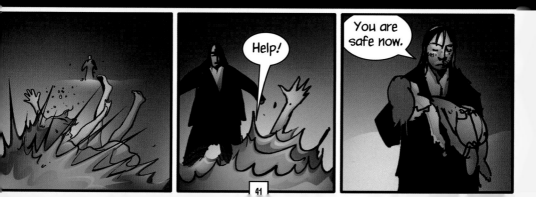

Help!

You are safe now.

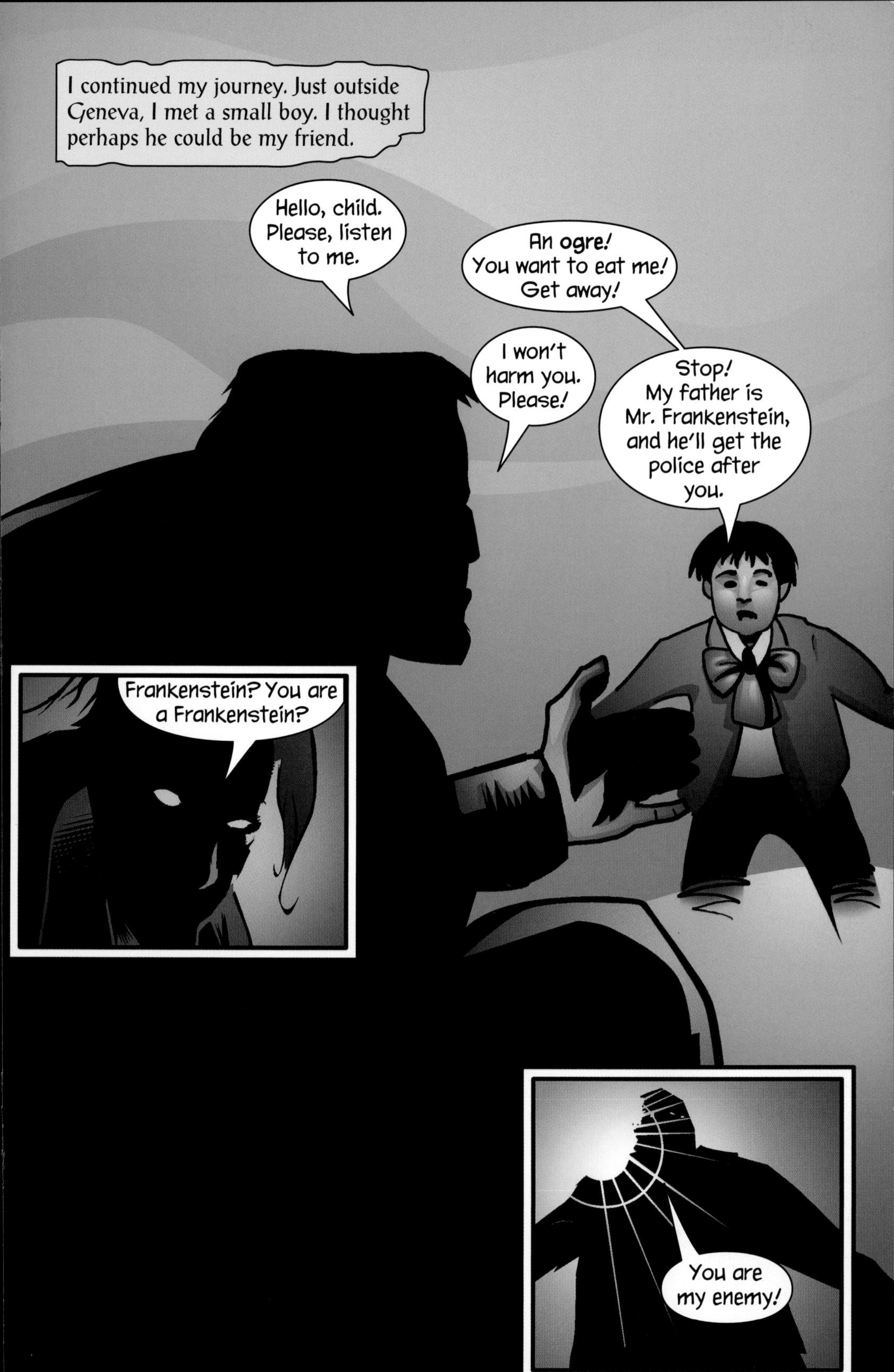
I continued my journey. Just outside Geneva, I met a small boy. I thought perhaps he could be my friend.
Hello, child. Please, listen to me.
An ogre! You want to eat me! Get away!
I won't harm you. Please!
Stop! My father is Mr. Frankenstein, and he'll get the police after you.
Frankenstein? You are a Frankenstein?
You are my enemy!

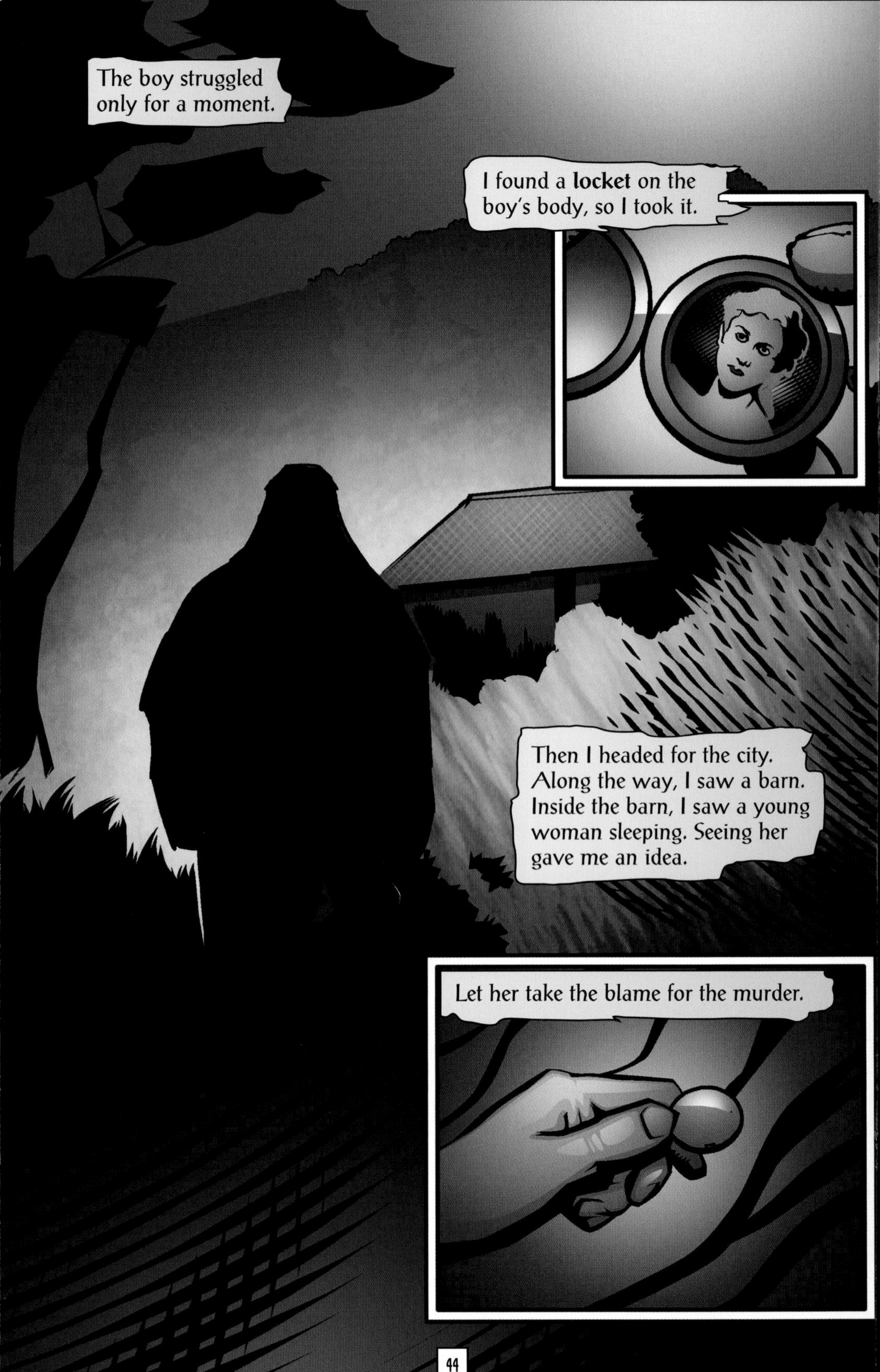
The boy struggled only for a moment.
I found a **locket** on the boy's body, so I took it.
Then I headed for the city. Along the way, I saw a barn. Inside the barn, I saw a young woman sleeping. Seeing her gave me an idea.
Let her take the blame for the murder.

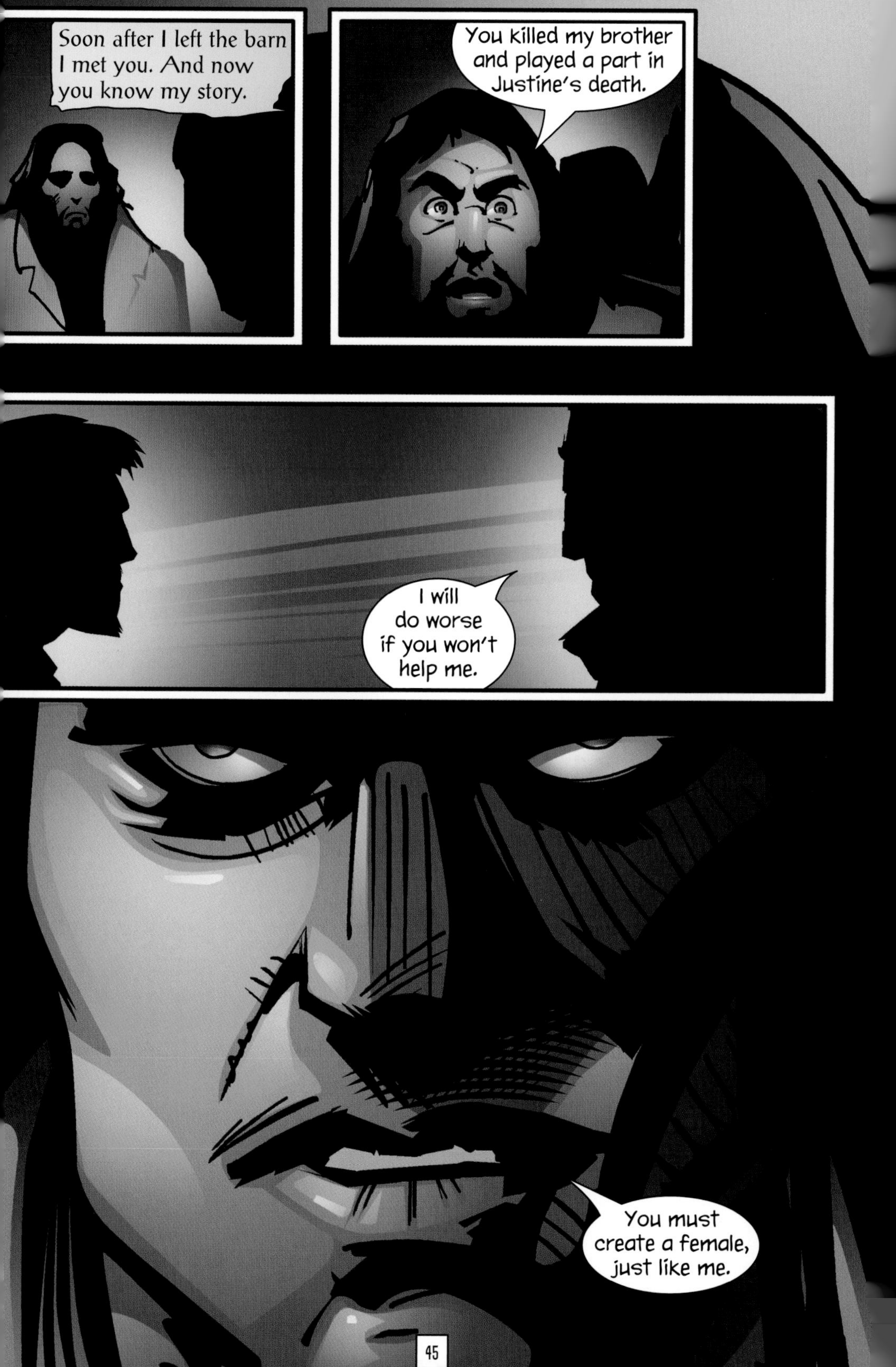
Soon after I left the barn I met you. And now you know my story.
You killed my brother and played a part in Justine's death.
I will do worse if you won't help me.
You must create a female, just like me.

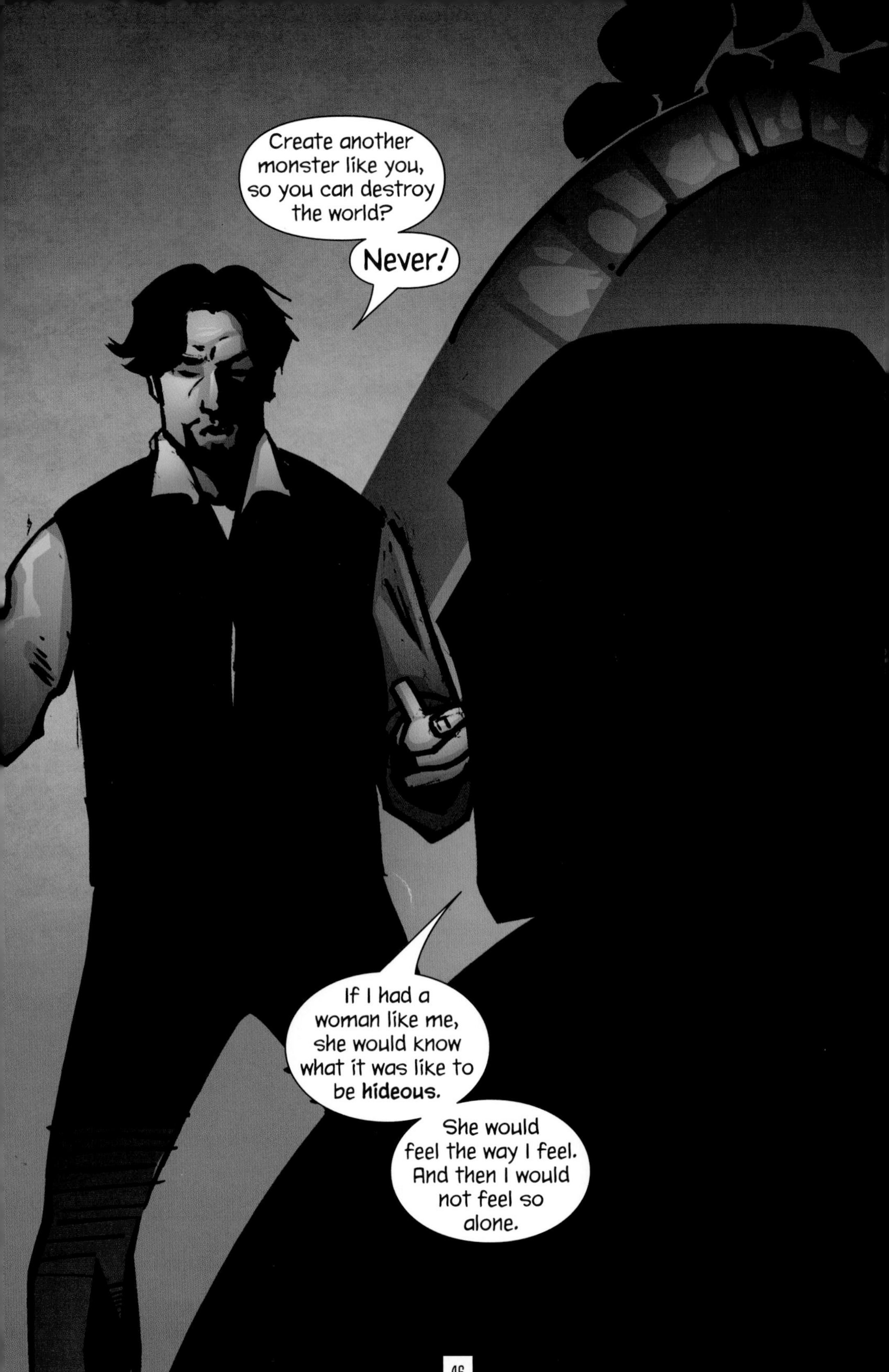
Create another monster like you, so you can destroy the world?
Never!
If I had a woman like me, she would know what it was like to be **hideous**.
She would feel the way I feel. And then I would not feel so alone.

CHAPTER 4
A BROKEN PROMISE

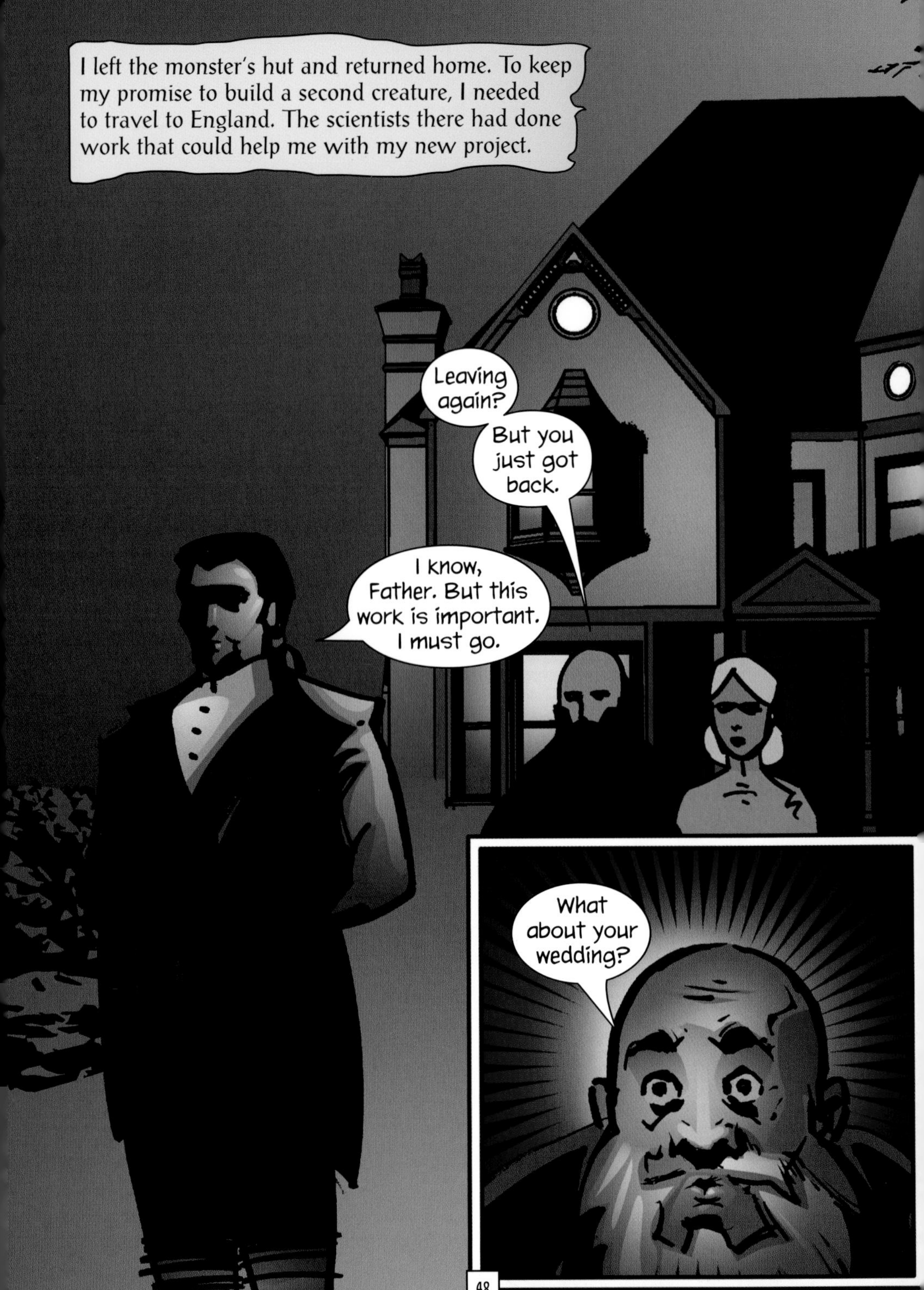

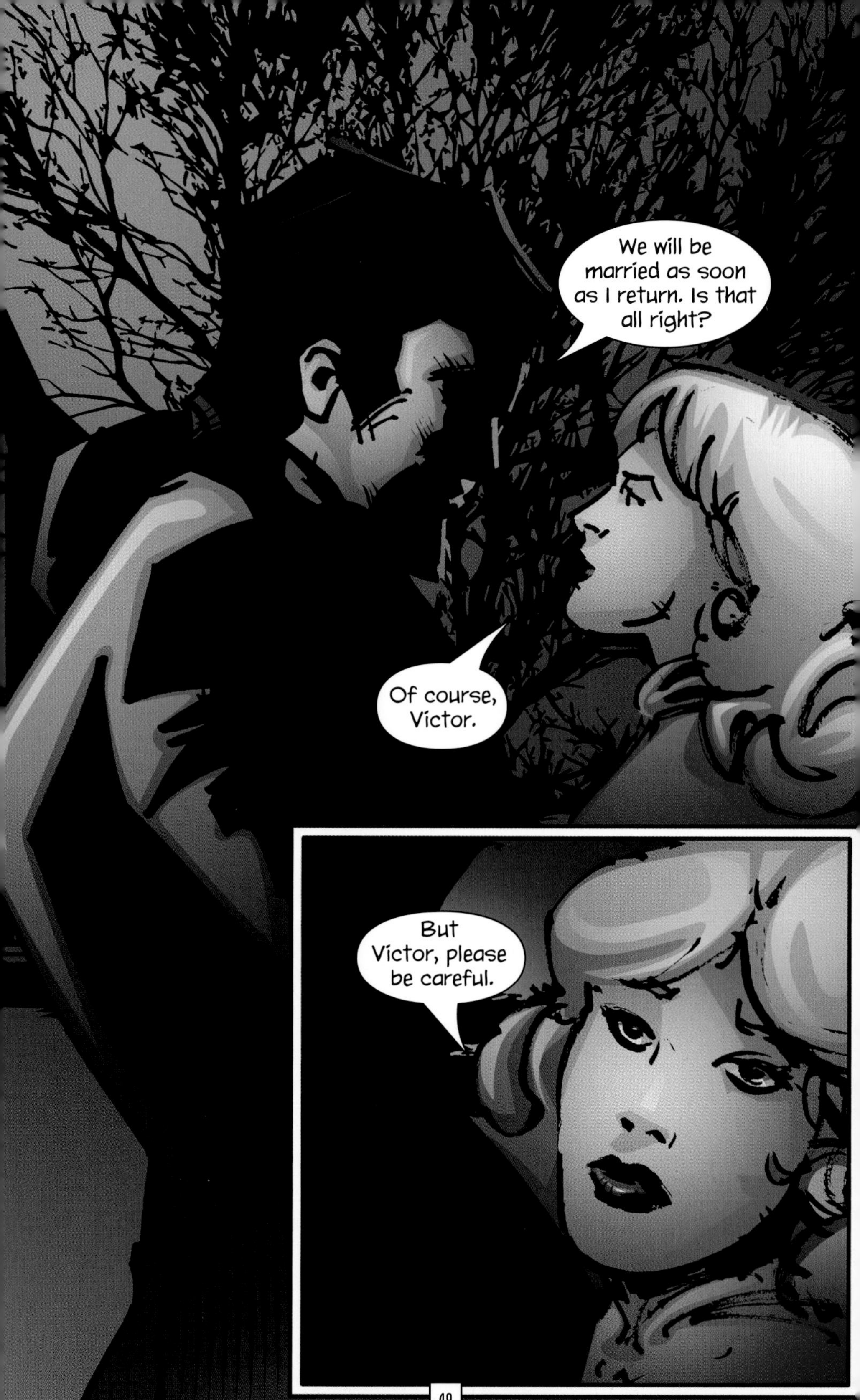
We will be married as soon as I return. Is that all right?
Of course, Victor.
But Victor, please be careful.

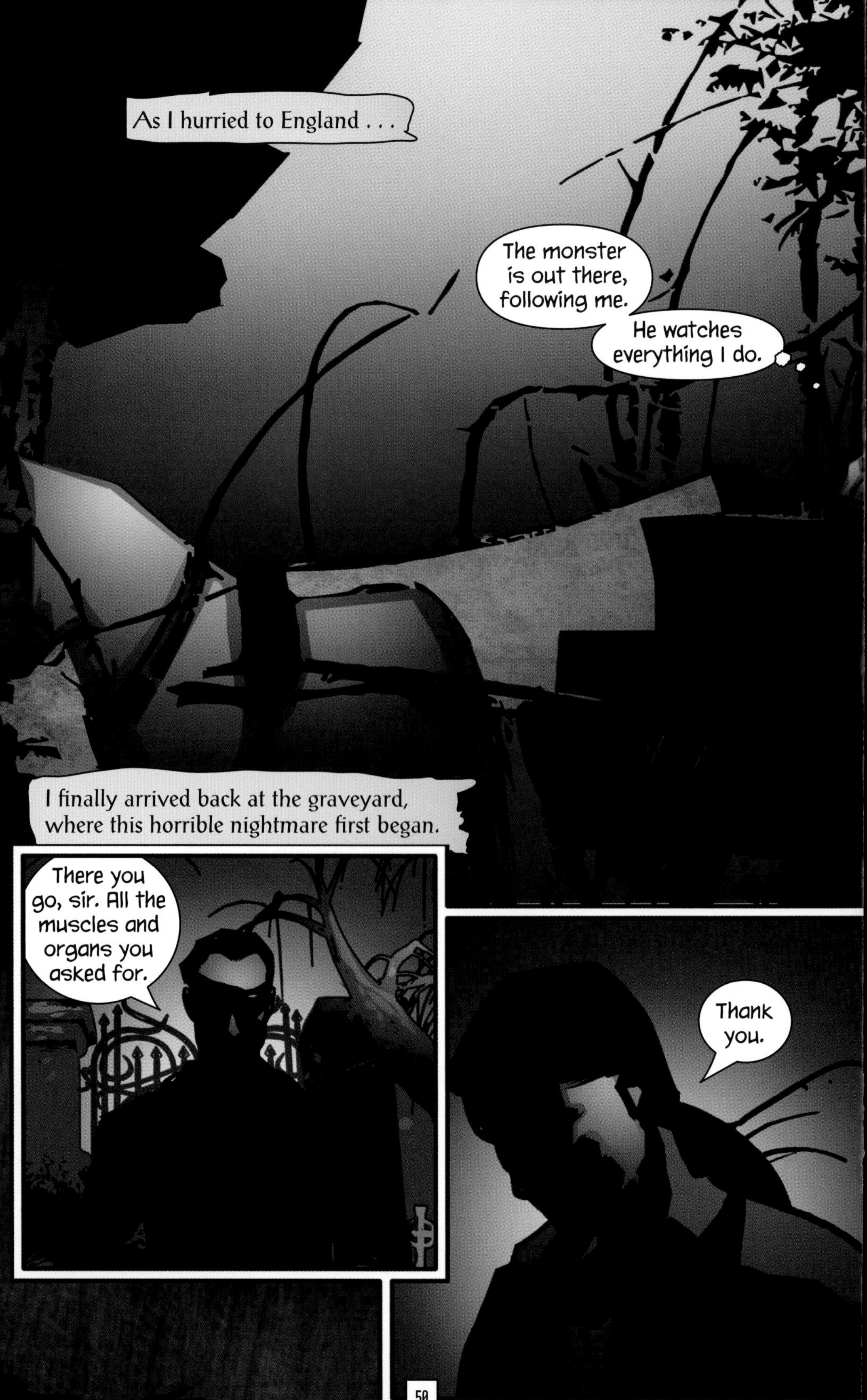
As I hurried to England . . .
The monster is out there, following me.
He watches everything I do.
I finally arrived back at the graveyard, where this horrible nightmare first began.
There you go, sir. All the muscles and organs you asked for.
Thank you.

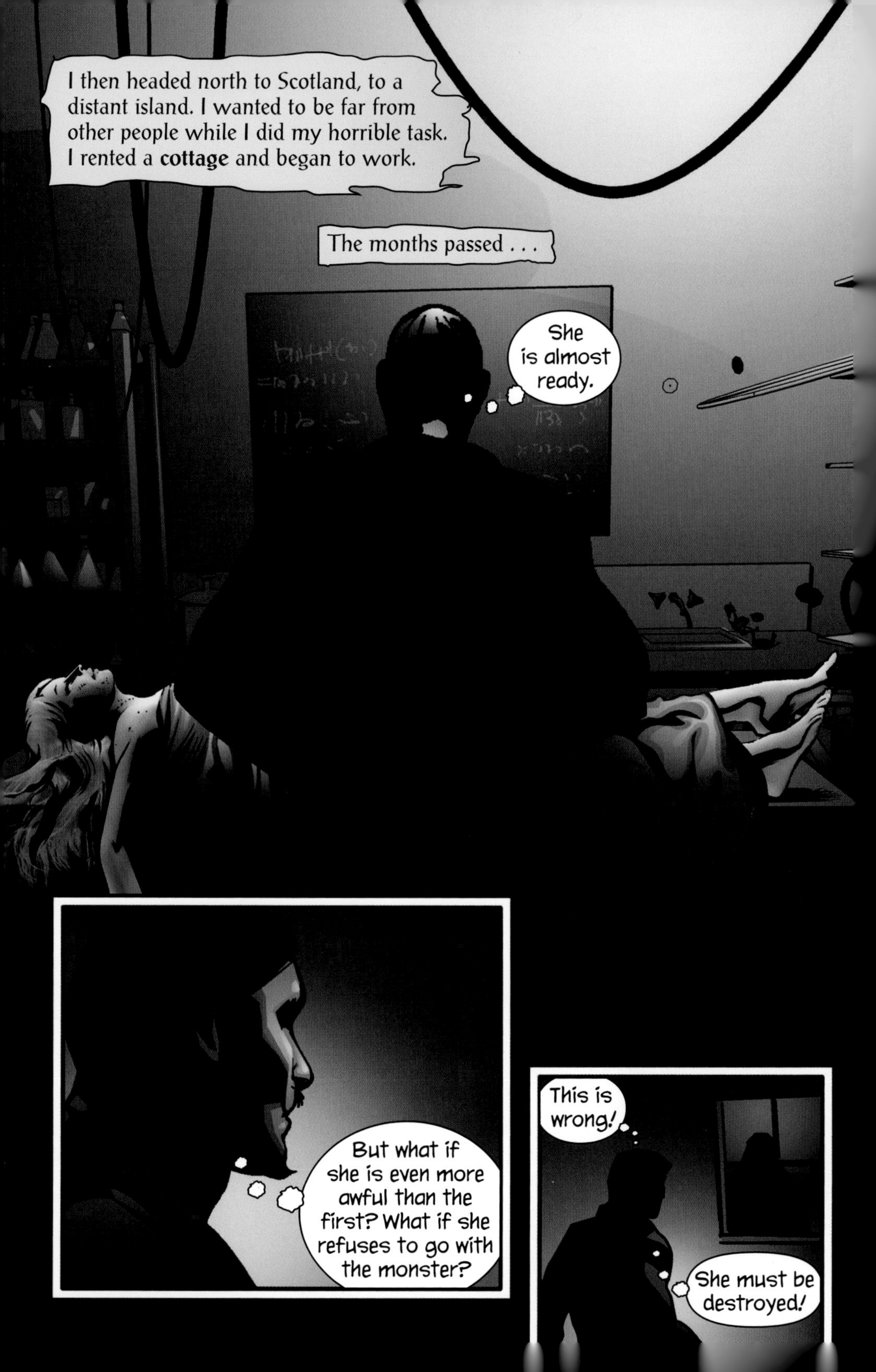
I then headed north to Scotland, to a distant island. I wanted to be far from other people while I did my horrible task. I rented a **cottage** and began to work.
The months passed . . .
She is almost ready.
But what if she is even more awful than the first? What if she refuses to go with the monster?
This is wrong!
She must be destroyed!

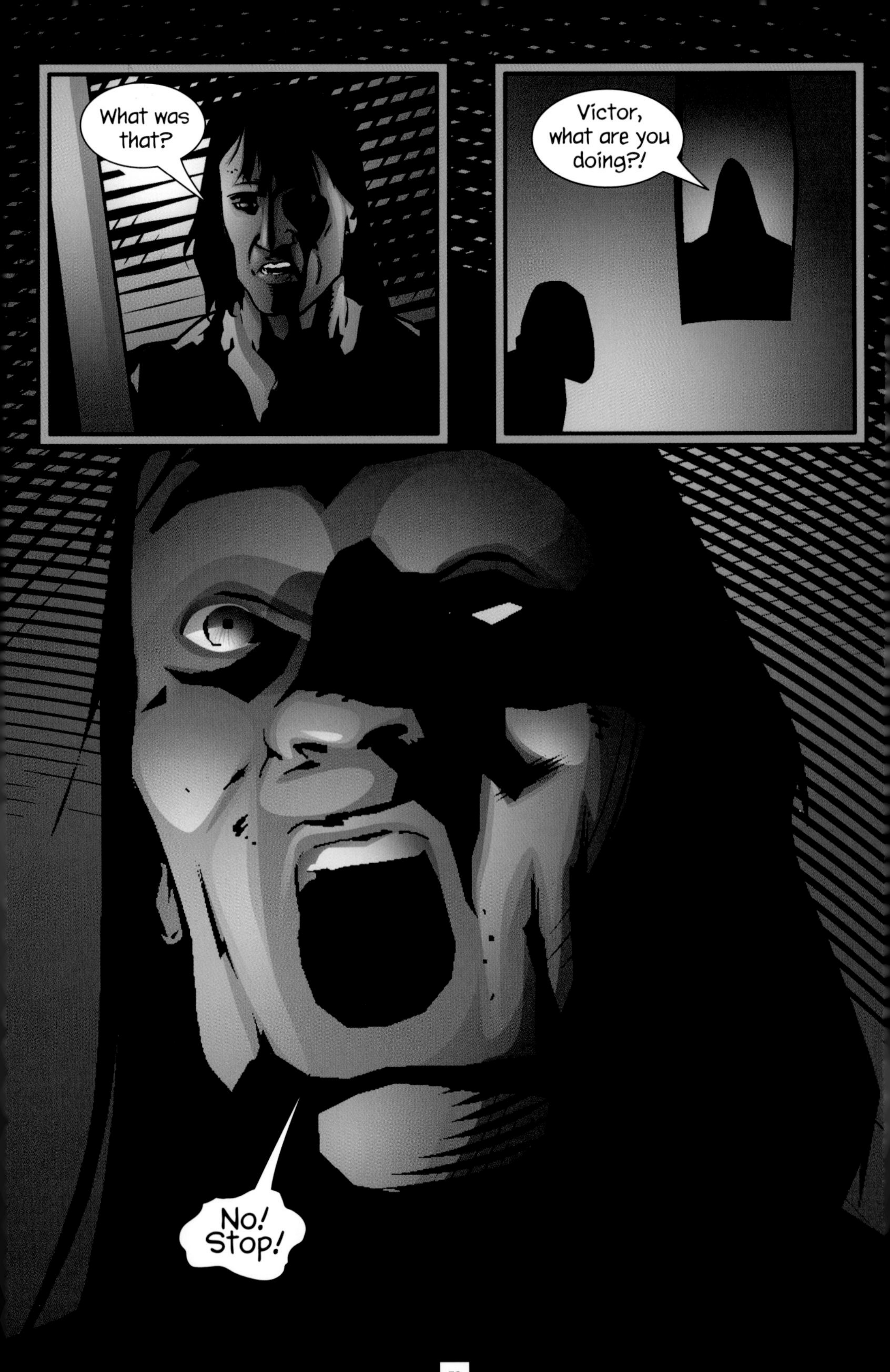
What was that?
Victor, what are you doing?!
No! Stop!

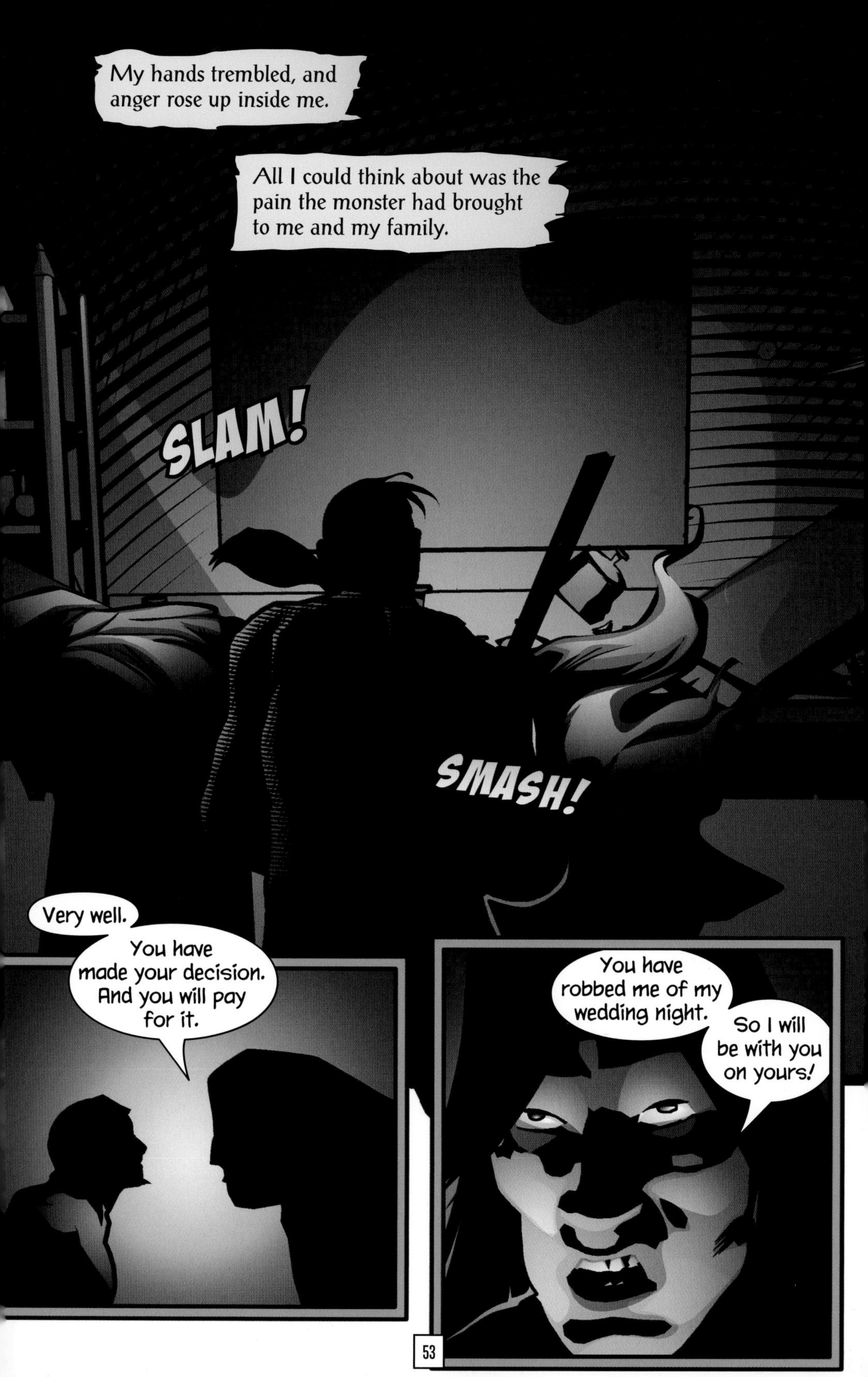

My hands trembled, and anger rose up inside me.
All I could think about was the pain the monster had brought to me and my family.
SLAM!
SMASH!
Very well.
You have made your decision. And you will pay for it.
You have robbed me of my wedding night.
So I will be with you on yours!

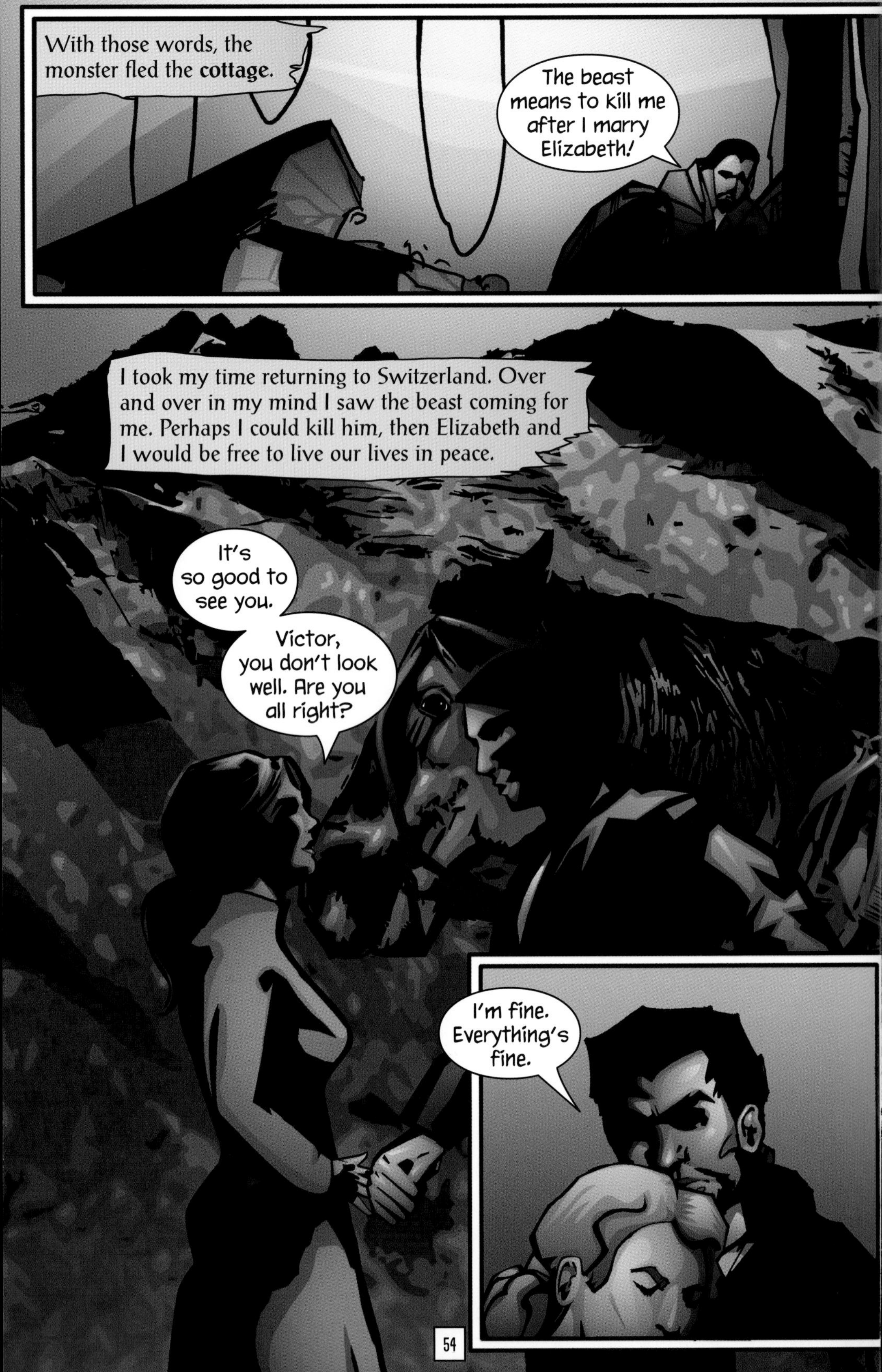
With those words, the monster fled the **cottage**.
The beast means to kill me after I marry Elizabeth!
I took my time returning to Switzerland. Over and over in my mind I saw the beast coming for me. Perhaps I could kill him, then Elizabeth and I would be free to live our lives in peace.
It's so good to see you.
Victor, you don't look well. Are you all right?
I'm fine. Everything's fine.

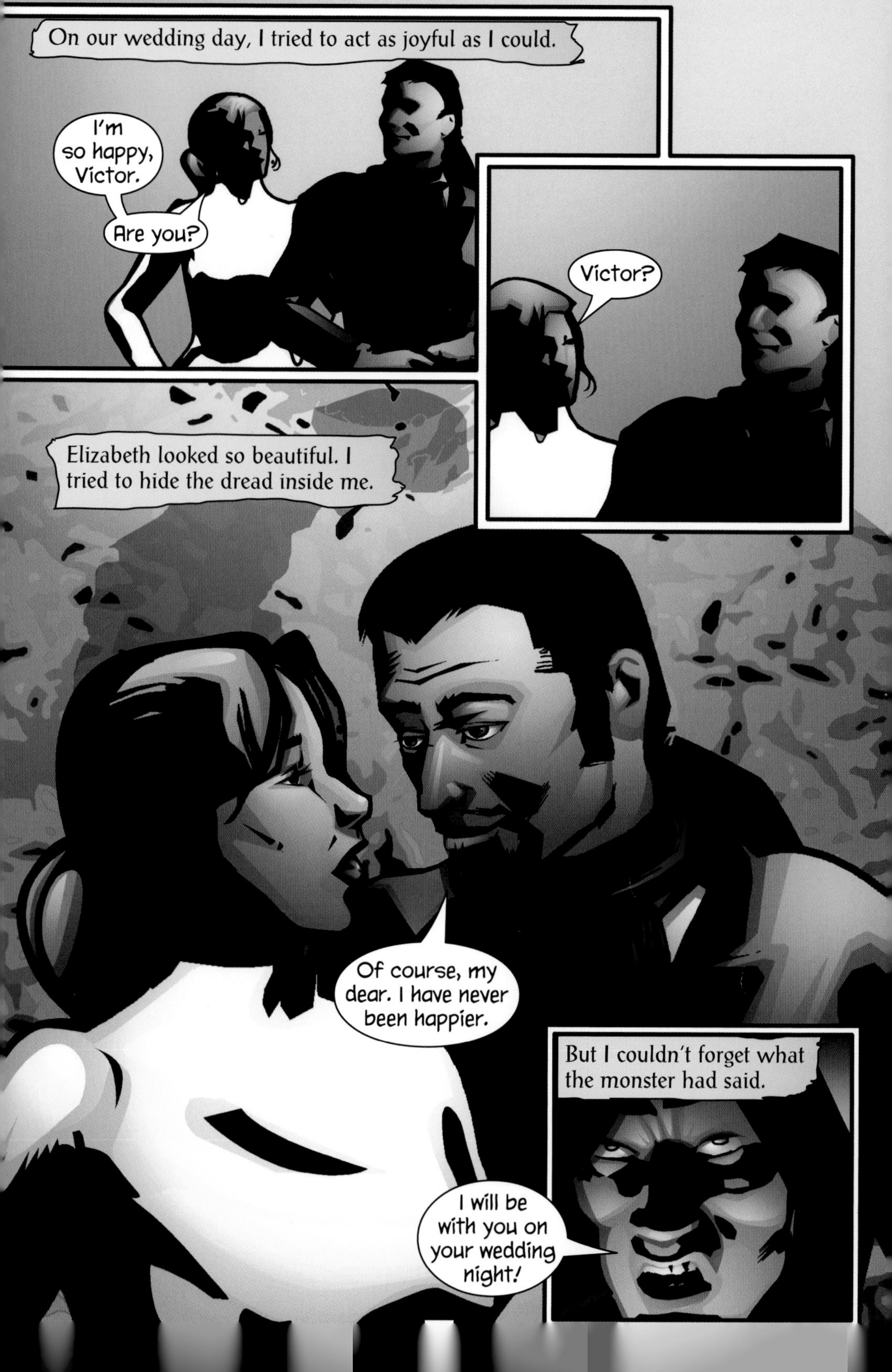
On our wedding day, I tried to act as joyful as I could.
I'm so happy, Victor.
Are you?
Victor?
Elizabeth looked so beautiful. I tried to hide the dread inside me.
Of course, my dear. I have never been happier.
But I couldn't forget what the monster had said.
I will be with you on your wedding night!

CHAPTER 5
THE END OF FRANKENSTEIN

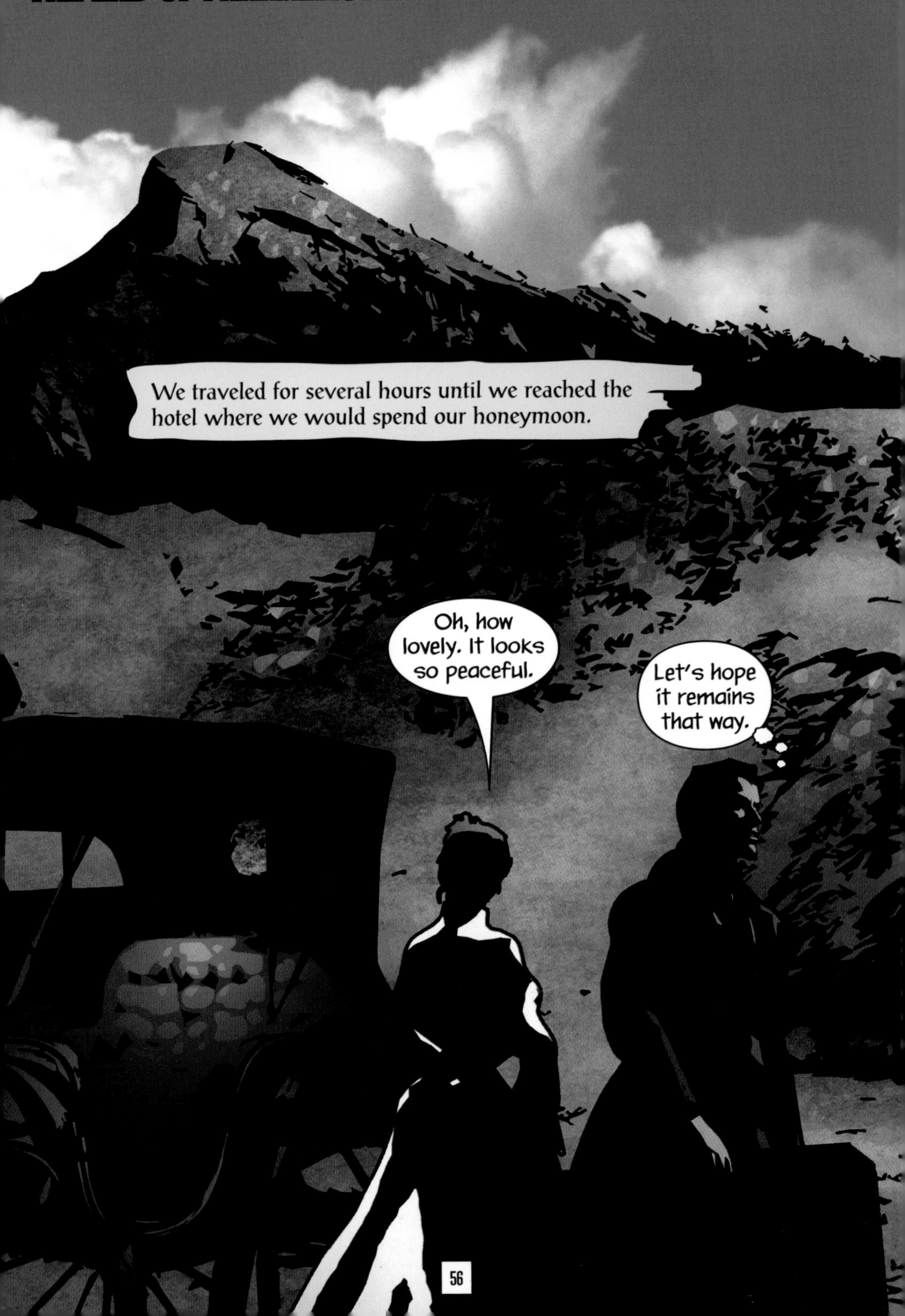
We traveled for several hours until we reached the hotel where we would spend our honeymoon.
Oh, how lovely. It looks so peaceful.
Let's hope it remains that way.

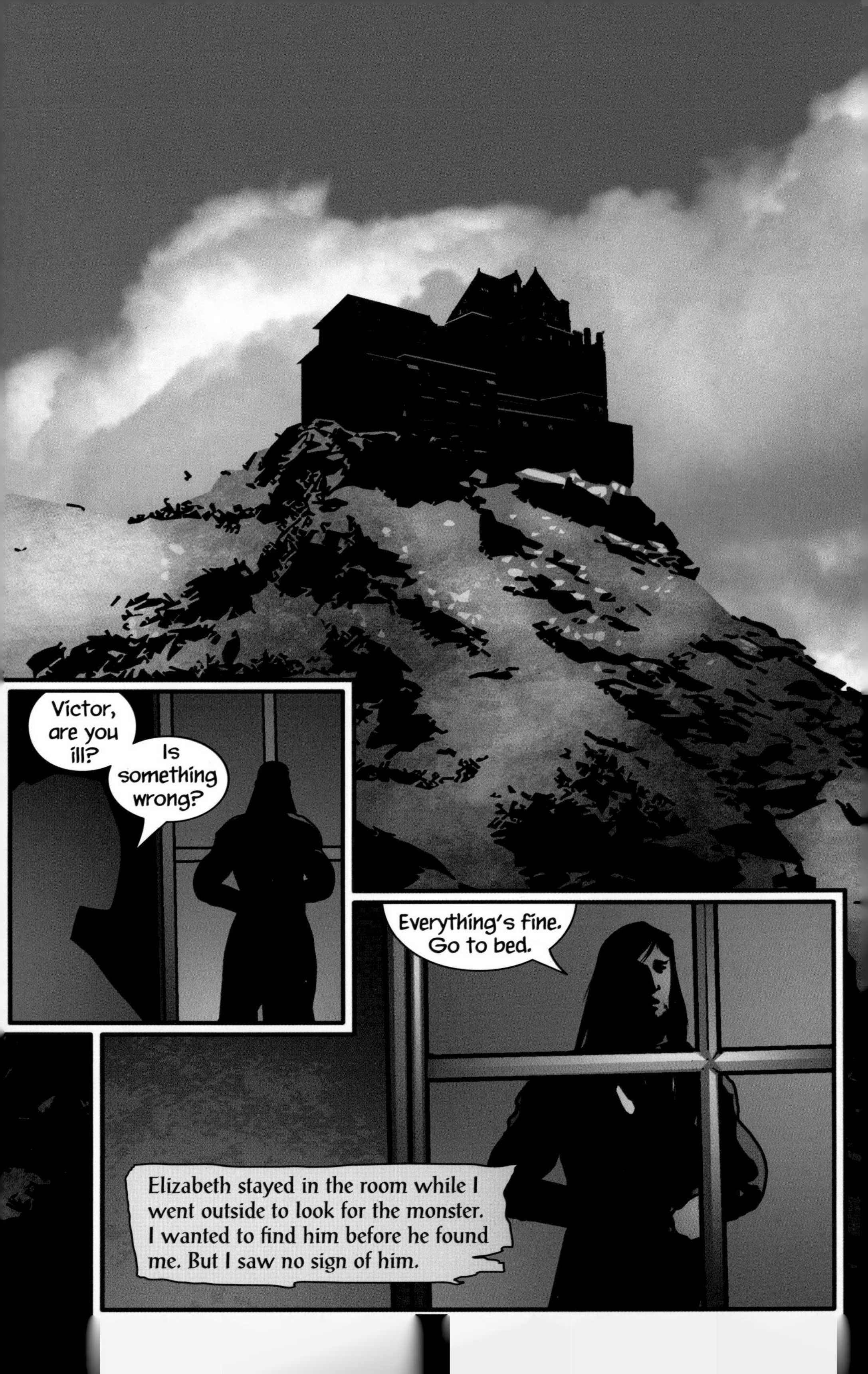
Victor, are you ill?
Is something wrong?
Everything's fine. Go to bed.
Elizabeth stayed in the room while I went outside to look for the monster. I wanted to find him before he found me. But I saw no sign of him.

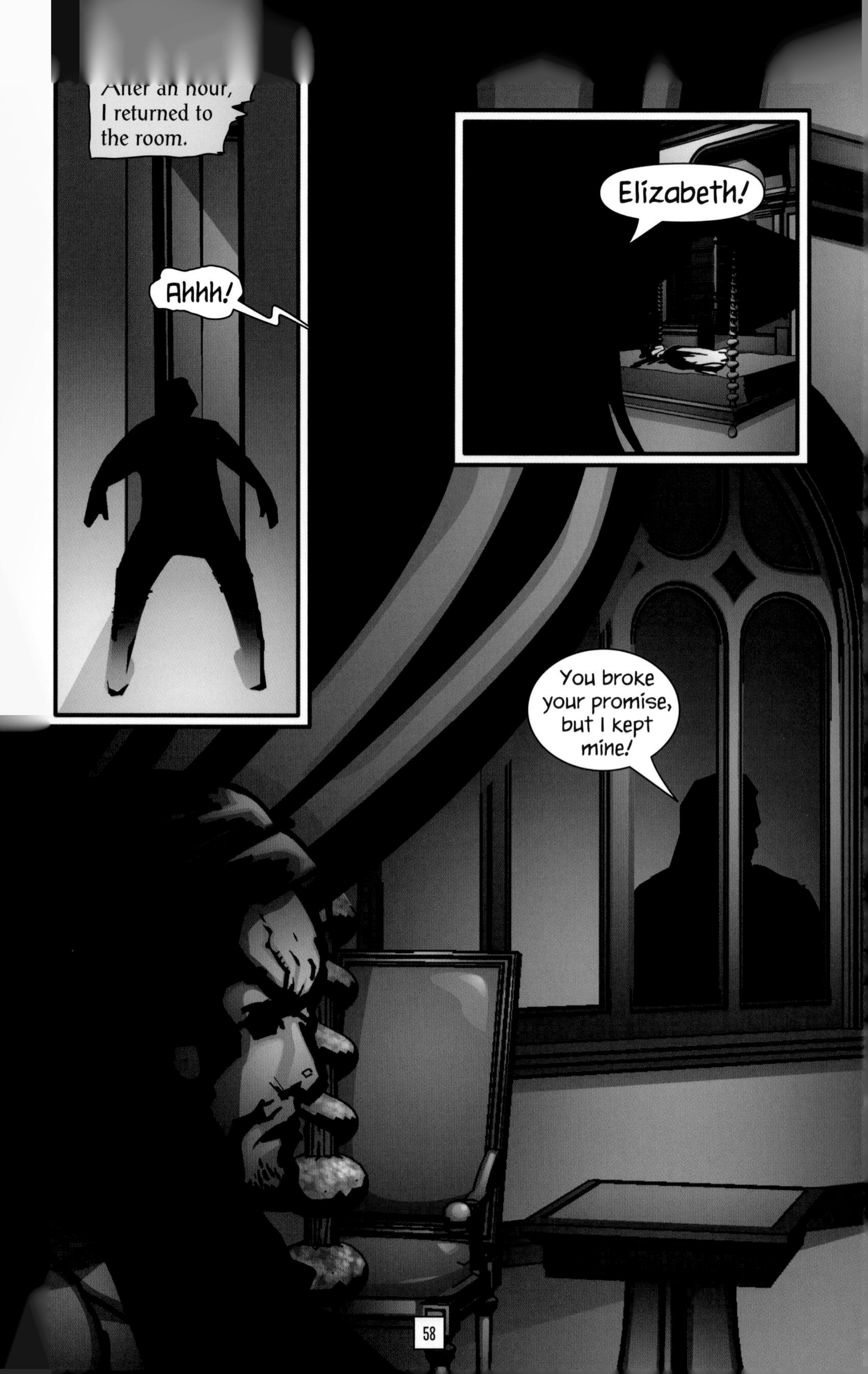
After an hour,
I returned to the room.
Ahhh!
Elizabeth!
You broke your promise, but I kept mine!

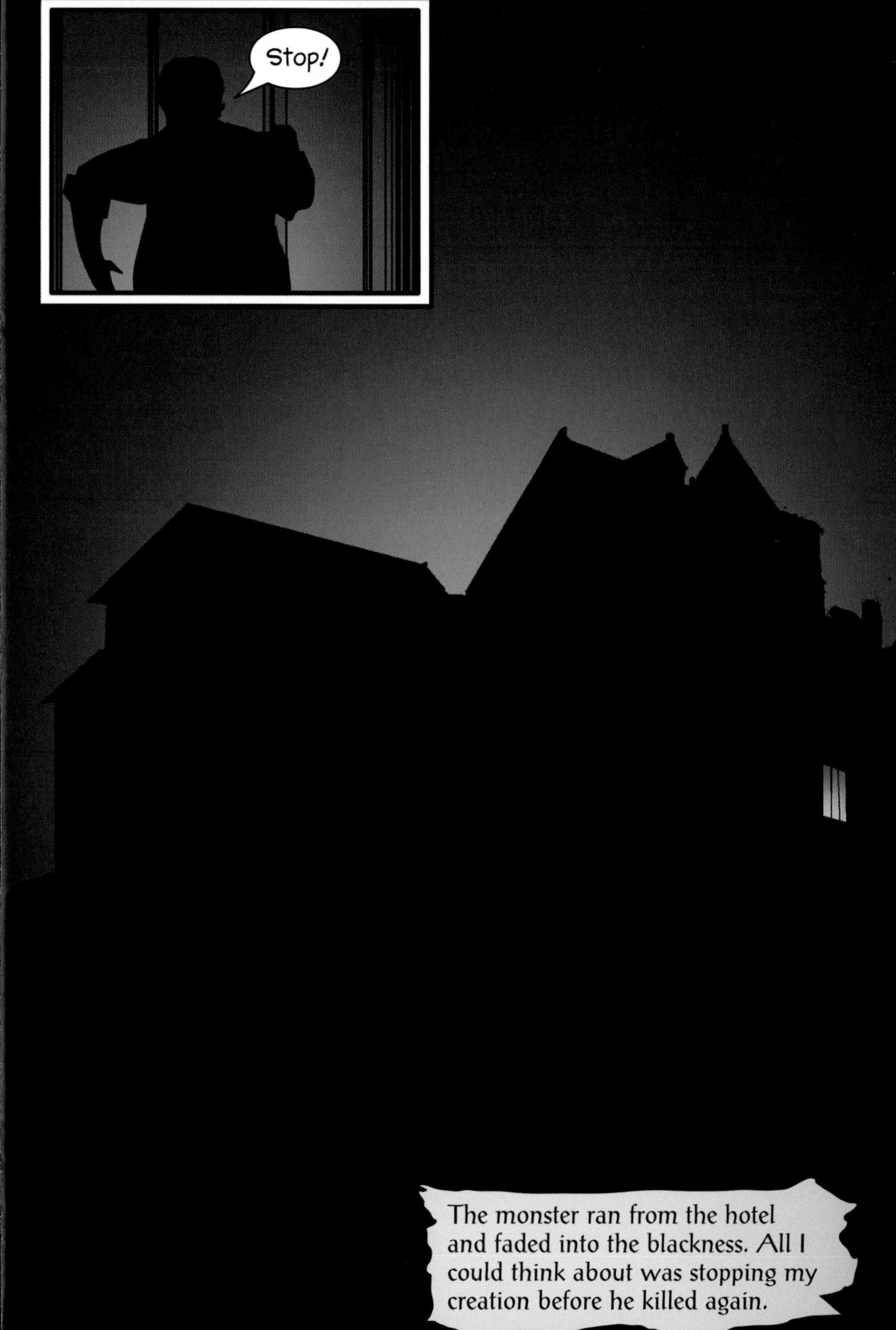
Stop!
The monster ran from the hotel and faded into the blackness. All I could think about was stopping my creation before he killed again.

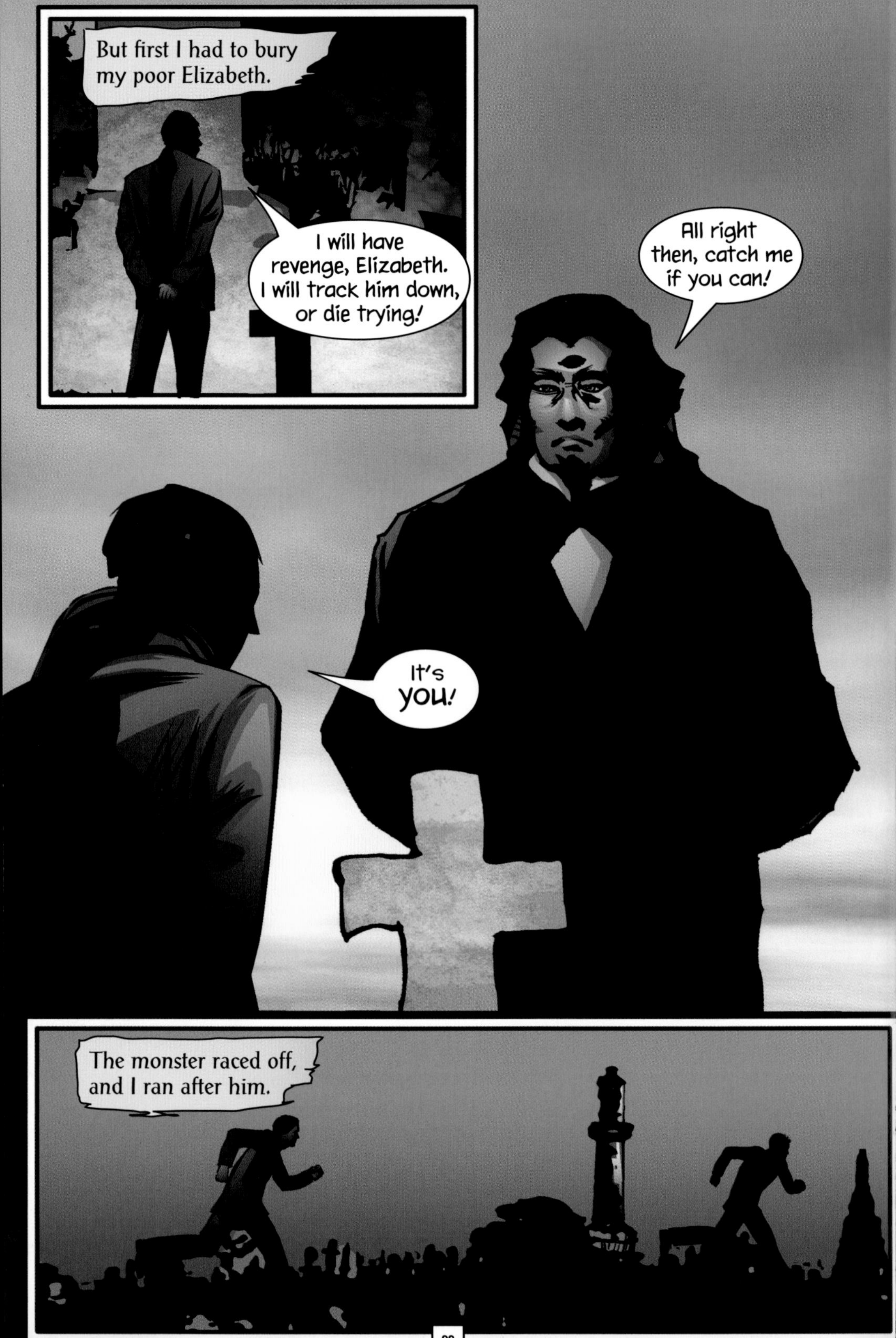
But first I had to bury my poor Elizabeth.
I will have revenge, Elizabeth. I will track him down, or die trying!
All right then, catch me if you can!
It's you!
The monster raced off, and I ran after him.

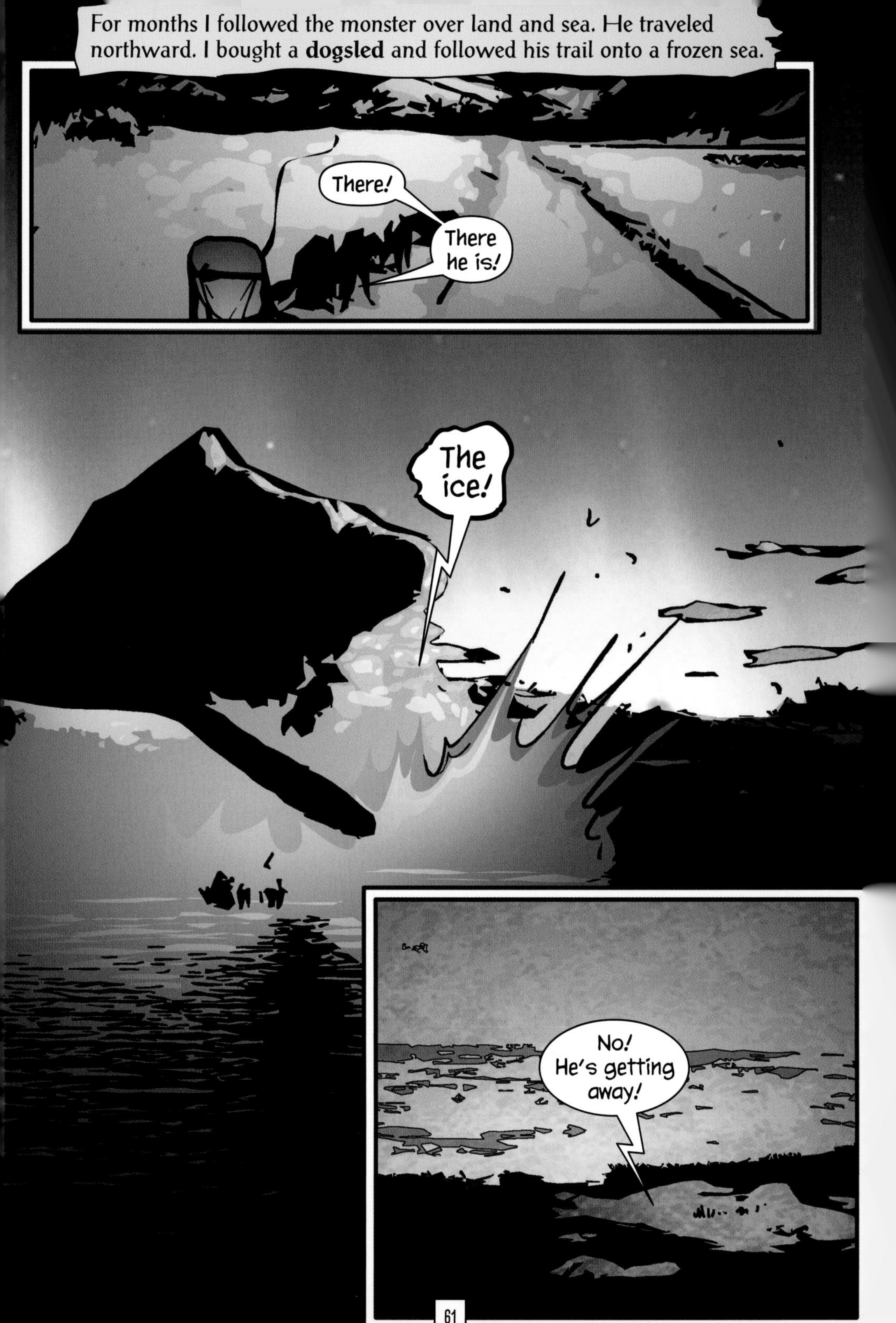
For months I followed the monster over land and sea. He traveled northward. I bought a **dogsled** and followed his trail onto a frozen sea.
There!
There he is!
The ice!
No! He's getting away!

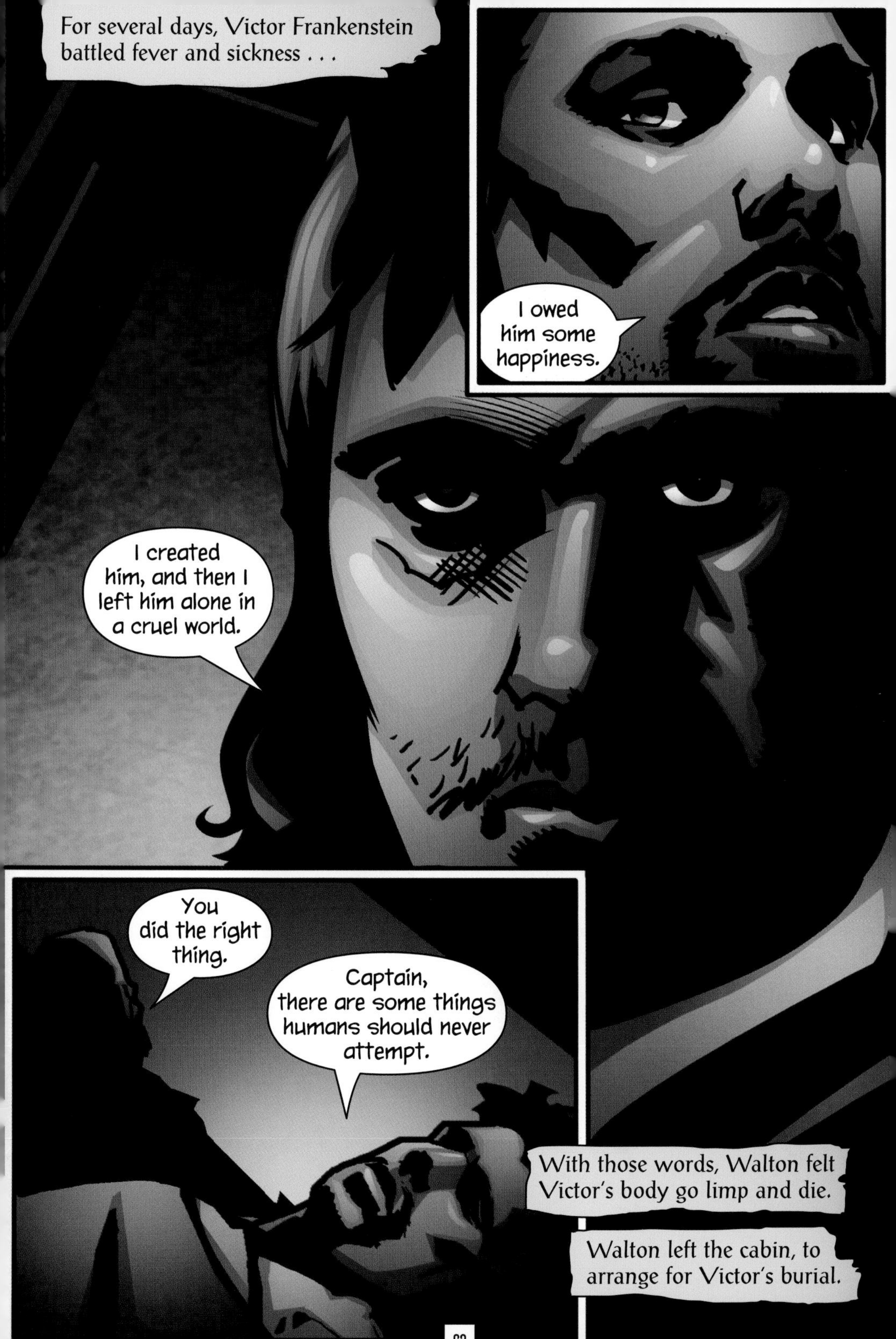
For several days, Victor Frankenstein battled fever and sickness . . .
I owed him some happiness.
I created him, and then I left him alone in a cruel world.
You did the right thing.
Captain, there are some things humans should never attempt.
With those words, Walton felt Victor's body go limp and die.
Walton left the cabin, to arrange for Victor's burial.

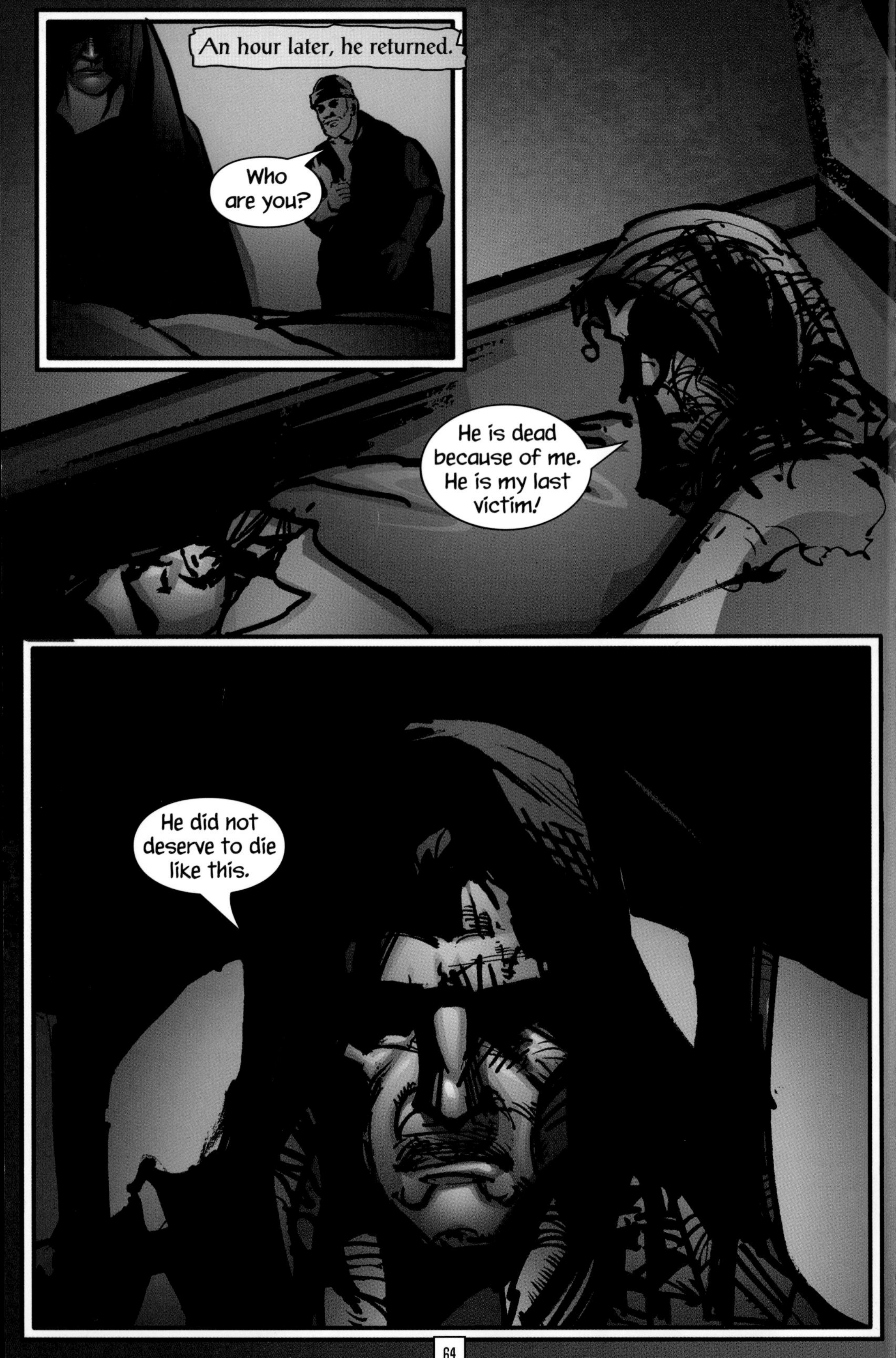
An hour later, he returned.
Who are you?
He is dead because of me. He is my last victim!
He did not deserve to die like this.

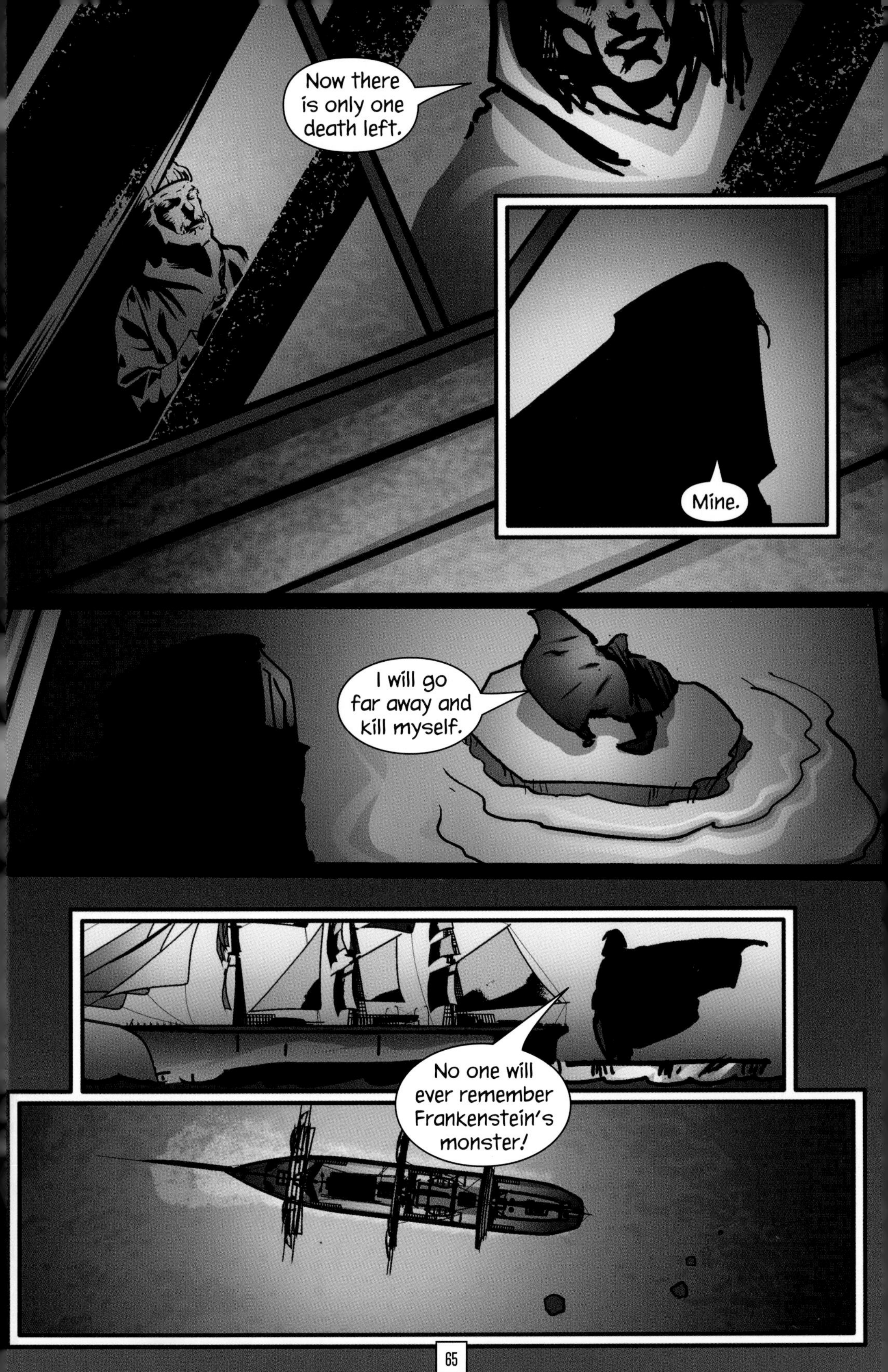
Now there is only one death left.
Mine.
I will go far away and kill myself.
No one will ever remember Frankenstein's monster!

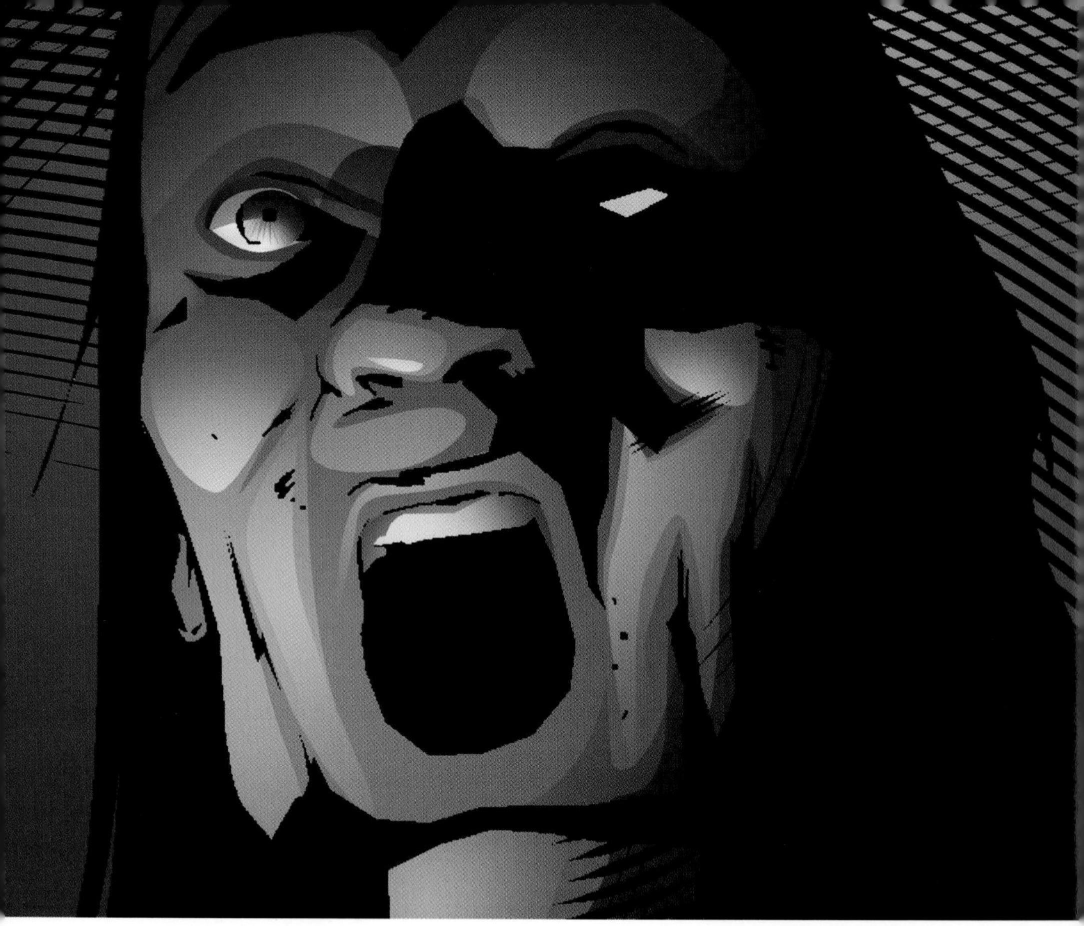

ABOUT THE RETELLING AUTHOR AND ILLUSTRATOR

Michael Burgan has written many fiction and nonfiction books for children. A history graduate from the University of Connecticut, Burgan worked at *Weekly Reader* for six years before beginning his freelance career. He has received an award from the Educational Press Association of America and has won several playwriting contests. He lives in Chicago with his wife, Samantha.

Dennis Calero has illustrated book covers, comic books, and role-playing games for many years. He has done work for companies such as Marvel, DC Comics, White Wolf, Wizards of the Coast, and Capstone.

GLOSSARY

alchemists (AL-kem-ists)—persons who practice the ancient science known as alchemy (AL-kem-ee). These scientists seek to turn metal into gold, discover a cure for disease, and develop medicine for people to live forever.

Arctic Circle (ARK-tik SUR-kuhl)—an area circling the northern part of the earth, where temperatures are extremely cold

cottage (KOT-ij)—a small house in the country

dogsled (DAWG-sled)—a sled pulled by dogs, used for traveling over ice and snow

floes (FLOWZ)—large sheets of floating ice

hideous (HID-ee-uhss)—horribly ugly

locket (LOK-it)—a small piece of jewelry that usually hangs from a necklace and can hold a photograph or other small item

ogre (OH-gur)—an ugly giant in fairy tales that feeds on human beings

potion (POH-shuhn)—a mixture of liquids

COMMON CORE ALIGNED
READING QUESTIONS

1. Both Frankenstein and his monster serve as narrators in this book. Compare and contrast their similarities and differences as narrators. (*"Compare and contrast the point of view from which different stories are narrated."*)

2. True or false: Frankenstein is the name of the monster. Explain your answer using an example from the text. (*"Refer to details and examples in a text when explaining what the text says explicitly and when drawing inferences from the text."*)

3. What happens to Victor Frankenstein on his wedding night? Identify a page where the events unfold, then explain them in your own words. (*"Describe in depth a character . . . drawing on specific details in the text."*)

4. Learning is a significant theme in this graphic novel. Why? Which characters engage in learning activities? Find specific pages, panels, and/or words to support your thoughts. (*"Determine a theme of a story."*)

5. Can you find three examples of words and/or images to describe the ending of this story? (*"Explain major differences between . . . structural elements."*)

COMMON CORE ALIGNED
WRITING QUESTIONS

1. If you were a narrator for this story, what would you want to tell the reader about the events? What perspective would you take? One from a minor character? A new character? *("Orient the reader by establishing a situation and introducing a narrator.")*

2. In your opinion, who is the hero and who is the villain in Mary Shelley's *Frankenstein*? Be sure to include images, words, events, etc. from the story that support your argument. *("Write opinion pieces on topics or texts, supporting a point of view with reasons and information.")*

3. Write a short essay that summarizes *Frankenstein* for someone who hasn't read this graphic novel. Using evidence from the story, what happens, and when? *("Draw evidence from literary . . . texts to support analysis.")*

4. Reread a few pages of *Frankenstein* each day, and keep a journal that focuses on your thoughts about each page you read. *("Write routinely over extended time frames.")*

5. One of the most important themes in *Frankenstein* is responsibility. In your opinion, which character, event, or situation best explores the idea of being responsible? Provide a clearly stated opinion and an organizational structure to support your opinion. *("Produce clear and coherent writing in which the development and organization are appropriate to task, purpose, and audience.")*

READ THEM ALL!

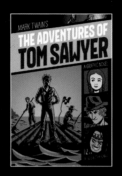

JULES VERNE'S
20,000 LEAGUES UNDER THE SEA
A GRAPHIC NOVEL

MARK TWAIN'S
THE ADVENTURES OF TOM SAWYER
A GRAPHIC NOVEL

ANNA SEWELL'S
BLACK BEAUTY
A GRAPHIC NOVEL

VICTOR HUGO'S
THE HUNCHBACK OF NOTRE DAME
A GRAPHIC NOVEL

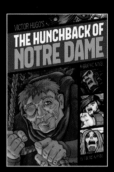

ROBIN HOOD
A GRAPHIC NOVEL

ROBERT LOUIS STEVENSON'S
TREASURE ISLAND
A GRAPHIC NOVEL

MARY SHELLEY'S
FRANKENSTEIN
A GRAPHIC NOVEL

JULES VERNE'S
JOURNEY TO THE CENTER OF THE EARTH
A GRAPHIC NOVEL

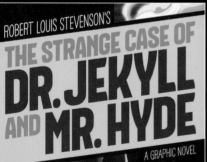

ROBERT LOUIS STEVENSON'S
THE STRANGE CASE OF DR. JEKYLL AND MR. HYDE
A GRAPHIC NOVEL

BY BOWEN & FERRAN

WASHINGTON IRVING'S
THE LEGEND OF SLEEPY HOLLOW
A GRAPHIC NOVEL

BRAM STOKER'S
DRACULA

JONATHAN SWIFT'S
GULLIVER'S TRAVELS
A GRAPHIC NOVEL

ARTHUR CONAN DOYLE'S
THE HOUND OF THE BASKERVILLES
A GRAPHIC NOVEL

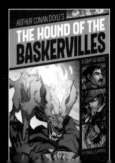

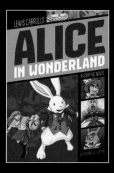
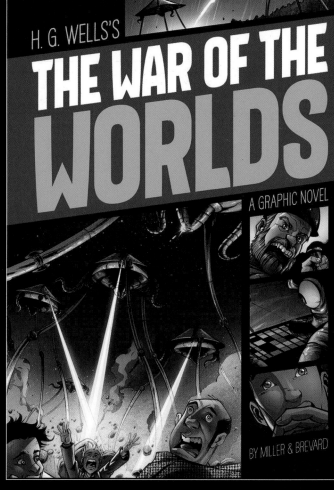
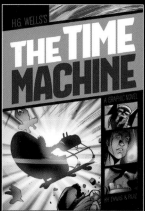
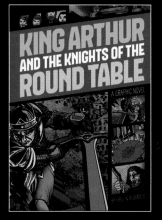
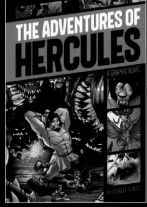